Lord of the Nile

Black Panther Series, Volume 1

Patricia Simpson

Published by Patricia Simpson, 2023.

LORD OF THE NILE

First edition. March 25, 2023.

ISBN: 978-1735082820

Written by Patricia Simpson.

Also by Patricia Simpson

Black Panther Series
Lord of the Nile

The Londo Chronicles
Apothecary
Phoenix
Prodigy

Watch for more at https://patriciasimpson.com.

Table of Contents

To BB--

Bubbles are a girl's best friend.

Chapter One

Baltimore, Maryland, 1994

B The bell on the shop door tinkled too soon. Surprised, Karissa Spencer looked up from the lioness she was sculpting. She glanced over the railing of the loft to the gallery below, wondering if her partner, Josh Lambert, had come back prematurely from his dinner run. The large gallery was bathed in shadows and the lights on the sculptures and paintings were nearly swallowed by the darkness. As far as she could tell, no one was there. But then, why had the bell rung?

All was quiet—too quiet—which was unlike Josh. He would have blustered into the shop, calling out to her and slamming the door behind him. Instead, the room below remained still and dark. Ill at ease–but not sure why–Karissa picked up her sculpting knife and slipped off her stool.

"Who's there?" she called, making sure her voice sounded clear and strong.

She walked to the railing and looked down. A slight movement caught her eye. She glanced at the pedestal that displayed a bronze of a panther and studied the darkness beyond it. There in the shadows was a pair of golden-brown eyes staring up at her, the same kind of eyes that had haunted her for more than a decade—the eyes of an Egyptian panther. Karissa felt a shiver of fear flash down her back.

Sixteen years ago, she had come face to face with an Egyptian panther and had been obsessed by the velvet power

1

of the big cat ever since. She tried to capture its essence in clay, in bronze, in paint, and in marble, but the feral spirit of the cat remained elusive, frustrating her.

No one else noticed the missing element. Her pieces sold as soon as she finished them and afforded her a decent living. In fact, her studio and gallery were going to be featured in an upcoming public television program called Women Artists in America. But Karissa knew something was lacking in her sculptures. Never once had she recreated the deadly power of the cat she had seen in Egypt.

Had her prodigious memory failed her, as it had failed to record a terrible night long ago? Or was she not gifted enough to capture the savage soul that smoldered in the eyes of the cat?

Yet here in her gallery were the same eyes, just as she remembered them, staring at her, chiding her for her human inadequacies.

"Ebony," a voice declared in a soft sweep of baritone tinged with a British accent.

"Pardon?" Karissa couldn't break away from those glowing eyes.

"If you would sculpt this in ebony, Miss Spencer, you would find satisfaction."

Ebony? She had never sculpted in wood, but she knew about ebony. The word derived from the Egyptian "hbny." It was a dark brown hardwood, almost black, easy to smooth and polish, and the perfect medium to accentuate the sinuous lines of a cat. Why hadn't she thought of trying ebony?

Karissa placed both hands on the rail and strained to see who spoke from the pool of darkness below.

"You seem to know me, sir. Have we met?"

"Once."

The voice was smooth and rich, and she felt the tone vibrate somewhere deep inside her, as if to dislodge a memory long forgotten. But she did not remember this man.

"A long time ago," he added.

"Oh?"

"Perhaps you will not recognize me as I am now." The man stepped away from the pedestal and into the light directed upon a freestanding bronze of three cats. He was dressed entirely in black—black shoes, slacks, and overcoat. Even his hair was black, swept off his forehead from a widow's peak and falling in slight waves to his collar. He was undeniably handsome, a bit older than she was—probably in his mid-thirties—with a strong pointed chin and neat ears close to his head. She would have remembered meeting such an attractive man and knew without a doubt that she had never laid eyes on him.

Karissa never forgot a face, literally. She possessed a photographic memory and could easily recall anything she read, heard or observed. According to her therapist, however, Karissa had chosen to lock some of her Egyptian memories away because they were too painful to look at. Until she brought them out and faced the truth, she would forever be missing one of the most significant times of her life—the day her father disappeared.

Karissa cut off all thoughts of her therapist and looked back at the man in the gallery. If he belonged to the missing part of her life, she wasn't about to admit it to him or spend any time searching for his face in the blank spot of her memory.

"I'm sorry but I don't recognize you," she replied.

"It was many years ago. In Egypt." He bowed almost imperceptibly. "I am called Mr. Asher."

"Mr. Asher." She inclined her head slightly in return. "Is there something I can do for you?"

"Yes?" he replied. "But may I come up?"

"I'll come down."

Karissa curved her fingers around the handle of the sculpting knife and descended the stairs, highly conscious of the stranger's regard. Mr. Asher was much taller than he first appeared once she gained the lowest step. He was half a foot taller than her five-foot-eight frame.

He looked down at her and smiled, never once breaking eye contact, and slowly raised the corners of his sensual mouth, appearing charming but cool at the same time. Not many men had the confidence or self-possession to meet a woman's eyes for such an extended length of time.

"What can I help you with?" She made a pretense of brushing something off the nearby bronze, so she didn't have to continue to meet his intense eyes. "Do you wish to look at something in particular?"

"Actually, yes. But not one of your fine pieces of art." He stepped closer. "I have been looking for you, Miss Spencer. For quite some time."

"Oh? Why?"

"You might possibly be the only one in the world who can help me find something."

"Find what?"

"A tomb."

She gave a half laugh. "I'm afraid you have the wrong Spencer. My father is the archaeologist, not me."

"Your father is no longer available. You are. And I know you saw the lost sphinx."

The lost sphinx.

Dread gripped her, constricting her breathing.

"No," she blurted. She turned away, fighting the urge to run back up the stairs and plunge into her work, just as she always did when bad memories threatened to overwhelm her.

"I know you remember the sphinx, Miss Spencer. The evidence is all over this gallery." He swept the air with a wave of his hand. He wore black gloves. "You do remember, don't you?"

"The only thing I remember about the sphinx is what people tell me."

"And what have they told you?"

"That because of the sphinx a curse was placed upon my family, which is why my mother got sick and died when I was twelve. And why my father apparently ran off, never to be heard from again. But I don't see how the sphinx concerns you, Mr. Asher."

"It concerns me very much. On a personal level."

She rolled the handle of the sculpting knife against her palm, not really frightened of Mr. Asher, but experiencing a great deal of disquiet, nonetheless. The topic of the sphinx was one she avoided. She decided to ask him to leave, but before she could form the words, Mr. Asher interrupted her.

"I have tried to locate you for many years, but you made the task very difficult. You changed your name for a period of time."

"I got married."

"Yes." His glance took in the rest of her figure and darted across the hand that clutched the knife. "But you are no longer married."

"My husband died four years ago."

"Was your marriage a happy one?"

"I don't see how that concerns you." She turned away so he couldn't see the emotions rushing across her face. A stranger had no right to ask such a personal question of her. "I think you'd better leave, Mr. Asher."

"Have I offended you?" he put in quietly, coming up behind her. "I was simply curious."

"My personal life is none of your business." She pivoted to head back to the stairs. "Good-bye, Mr. Asher."

"I will go as you request," he replied. "But first, spare a moment to hear my offer."

She put a hand on the stair rail, paused, and sighed. "What offer?"

"I will pay you a small fortune, Miss Spencer, if you will come to Egypt with me and help me locate the ruins of the sphinx. Where you saw the panther."

He knows about the panther.

She felt even more uneasy. She turned to face him but didn't look him in the eye. "Sorry, but I can't help you. I don't remember anything about that era in my life."

"You have a photographic memory, do you not?"

Karissa's glance rose to his handsome face, with its sharp, elegant nose and wide lower lip. "How do you know that about me?"

"I know much about you. As I said, I have been trying to find you for years."

"What else do you know?"

"I know about the circumstances of your husband's death."

She felt the color drop from her face. Her stomach clenched together. He couldn't possibly know about Thomas dying in bed with an eighteen-year-old girl. Karissa forced the hard knot inside to dissipate and vowed once again to avoid thinking about her philandering husband.

"Mr. Asher. I have nothing more to discuss with you." She motioned toward the door. "Please leave. Now."

He moved toward the door, his footfalls soundless. Not many people could walk so quietly across the oak parquet floor. At the door he turned. "Will you not consider my offer, Miss Spencer? It is very important."

"I don't accept offers from complete strangers. Especially offers that involve trips to foreign countries."

"I could make you a rich woman."

"By robbing graves? No thanks."

He stood in silence for a moment as if her words offended him. Then he put his hand on the doorknob. "My quest does not include stealing the possessions of the dead."

"What is your quest then?"

"To find a mummy of a certain woman and thereby repay a debt."

"That sounds noble, Mr. Asher, but highly suspicious."

"I assure you, my intentions are purely honorable."

"I'll bet." Karissa walked up a few steps. "Listen, Mr. Asher, I lost my father and mother to that sphinx. I have no desire to risk my life just to help your karmic credit rating."

"How may I change your mind?"

"You can't. Goodnight."

"You will find me persistent, Miss Spencer, for I must find the mummy as quickly as possible."

"If you harass me, Mr. Asher, you will find yourself arrested."

At that moment the door burst open, forcing Asher to step aside. Josh Lambert breezed in with a bag of Chinese food. "Dinner is served!" he announced before he noticed the dark visitor near the door.

"Sorry! Didn't see you there!" In his haste to retreat, Josh bumped into the corner of a pedestal behind him. The pedestal tipped, sending the marble figure of a cat toppling through the air. In a streak of black, Mr. Asher lunged to the side, caught the sculpture, and straightened, all in a single, fluid movement.

"No harm done," Asher replied. He adjusted the statue until it was shown to its best advantage in the light. Karissa was impressed not only by his quick reflexes and elegant self-control, but by his eye for the play of shadow and light on the stone.

Josh shot a questioning glance at Karissa.

Karissa paused, uncertain how to explain the visitor or his business. Not many people knew of her connection to Egypt, and she wasn't about to tell Josh of her troubled adolescence.

"If you will excuse me," Mr. Asher said, "I was just leaving."

He nodded slightly to both of them, and without making eye contact, walked out of the shop. Karissa watched him disappear into the night, as silently as he had come.

Josh raised his eyebrows. "Who in the heck was that?" he asked.

"Mr. Asher."

"Who's he?"

"I don't really know." Her voice trailed off, and she found it difficult to concentrate on what Josh was saying as he trotted past her up the stairs.

"Karissa, did you hear me?"

"Pardon?"

"I said, did you want the Kung Pao Chicken or the Mongolian Beef?"

"Oh, I don't care, Josh. Why don't we split them?"

As usual, he had bought twice as much food as they needed. His over-indulgence was not limited to food but concerned every facet of their business—from decorating the gallery to buying the latest computer equipment. Josh called his extravagances "investments in the future." Karissa called them just plain extravagances and knew the gallery could not sustain Josh's spending. The more pieces she sold, the more he spent, and she was tired of funding his spendthrift ways with her hard work. Josh had promised to cut back, but he lacked the self-discipline required to change his spending habits.

Shaking her head, Karissa gained the top of the stairs, went over to her worktable, and gazed down at the clay lioness she had been working on for a week. Ebony. Perhaps that was the secret to capturing the spirit of the cat. She would buy some ebony tomorrow and see what she could do with it. She put down the sculpting knife and joined Josh in the back room for dinner.

Two hours later, Karissa and Josh closed up and left for the evening. Karissa lived in a brownstone on Montgomery Street a half-mile away. On an ordinary day, she would walk along the avenue lined by historic homes and knobby hundred-year-old linden trees and use the time to decompress from her busy schedule. Tonight, however, Josh insisted on accompanying her. He turned the usual enjoyable stroll into a noisy parade, punctuated with jokes and late-breaking gossip about their patrons and clients.

At one time in her life Karissa had needed the jokes and the laughter. Josh had been a godsend then. Her heart had been heavy and troubled, and he had distracted her. Now she wanted more from a conversation than a good guffaw and more from a man than slapstick and bad puns. But Josh had no other way of interacting with the world. Worse, Josh seemed confident that he was the man for her, and no matter how many times she gently turned him away, he always bounced back, more certain than ever that she would agree to date him in the very near future.

More and more, Karissa found it impossible to work when Josh was around. She needed solitude, and Josh ignored her requests for peace and quiet. She knew it was time to sever their partnership in the gallery, but in order to do that she would need money to buy him out. And she just didn't have it. Most artists like herself did not make huge profits from their work—the ultimate sacrifice for having a career one truly enjoyed.

"As I was saying, Karissa—"

Josh broke off his monologue and stopped in his tracks.

Karissa stopped as well and glanced at him in surprise. "What's wrong?"

"They are." He nodded at the path ahead of them where three men in European-style business suits stood in front of a sedan that blocked the sidewalk.

Karissa surveyed the men in the light of the streetlamp. They were dark-skinned and had black hair and moustaches. Two of them were broad in the shoulders while the third man was short and slight.

"They're watching us," Josh said out of the side of his mouth. "And not in a good way."

"Why would they do that?"

"Who knows? I kind of doubt they're waiting to give us a lottery check. They just don't look the type."

"Let's cross the street," Karissa urged, "And see what they do."

Josh turned abruptly to head for the other side of the road, and Karissa hurried to catch up with him. She glanced over her shoulder at the men and saw one take a step toward them.

"They're coming!" she exclaimed.

Josh clutched her hand and set off at a quick walk. Karissa shot another glance backward and saw the thugs with the big shoulders trotting after them. Her heart pounded in alarm.

"Run," she cried, breaking from his grip.

She dashed back toward the gallery, sprinting along the sidewalk. Josh took a turn into an unfamiliar street, and she followed him up an alley. They ran along the narrow lane, dodging garbage cans and parked cars. But they didn't run fast enough. Soon Karissa heard the labored breathing of her pursuers close behind her. Adrenalin shot through her chest, overriding the sharp pain in her lungs as she sucked in gulps of air. She forced her legs to go faster.

Just as she thought she might outdistance the thugs, she tripped over a spade someone had left propped against a cement retaining wall. She landed on her shoulder and took the fall with a roll. But before she could get back up, one of the thugs grabbed her arm. He wrenched her to her feet.

"Got you!" he shouted, panting. He had wide gaps between his teeth and wore a heavy cologne that reminded her of the bazaars of Cairo.

Karissa yanked her arm back, but he held fast. "Josh!"

Josh skidded to a stop and turned around, just as the other man grabbed him.

The gap-toothed thug squeezed Karissa's upper arm. "You are to come with us. And if you cooperate, I will not have to hurt you."

Karissa stared at him, baffled that anyone would run her down like this. "Why me?" she asked.

"No questions."

"But—"

He slapped her across the face. "I said no questions!"

"Hey dude!" Josh exclaimed. "Don't go hitting her, or I'm warning you—"

"Shut up, American!" The gap-toothed thug pulled Karissa a few yards down the alley.

"What's it worth to you?" Josh demanded. "A couple hundred dollars? I can get you a couple hundred right now."

"Shut him up, Shamir," the gap-toothed man ordered.

Karissa held the side of her face, shocked by the man's brutal treatment of her. These men were dangerous. Were they connected to Mr. Asher? He said he was persistent. Would he resort to violence to get her back to Egypt?

The gap-toothed man dragged her toward the main street while Karissa struggled to see what Shamir was doing to Josh. To her horror, she saw Shamir hit him over the head with a gun. Josh crumpled to the ground. Then Shamir picked him up, strode to the nearest dumpster, and heaved Josh into the container. The cover clanged shut. Karissa prayed someone would hear all the noise and come to their assistance or at least call the police. But no one seemed to take notice of the action in the alley.

Her alarm deepened to terror.

"Help!" Karissa yelled.

Her captor clenched his nails into the flesh of her arm and drew a gun from his waistband.

"Shut up and quit struggling, or I'll do what Shamir did to your friend."

Karissa eyed the gun as it glinted in the darkness. Then she glanced down the alley where the big sedan waited for them.

"Let me go!" she twisted in his grip and ignored the flare of pain in her arm.

"I said shut up!" He raised the gun to strike her.

Desperate, she dug her heels into the gravel of the lane, refusing to be kidnapped, just as an unearthly snarl ripped through the night—a sound so foreign that all three of them froze in their tracks. Goose pimples flooded Karissa's skin as she turned in the direction of the snarl. She knew at once that the sound belonged to a big cat. But what was a big cat doing in the middle of Baltimore?

"Abdullah!" Shamir gasped. His voice was pinched with terror. "It is Lord Azhur!"

"Shut up!" Abdullah ordered, but his tone rose, shrill with fear.

Frantic, Karissa glanced at the face of her captor and saw that he had turned pale with horror.

A dark shape leaped from a high wall beside them and sailed through the air toward Abdullah. The man cried out, clutching at Karissa's arm, and nearly took her down with him as he crashed to the ground. Karissa struggled to keep on her feet as a streak of black landed in the alley. The streak morphed into the form of a huge cat that pinned Abdullah to the ground and then shook him by the nape of the neck until his spine snapped.

Terrified, Shamir staggered backward, holding his gun but shaking so hard he couldn't pull the trigger. In one magnificent movement, the cat bunched its flank muscles, soared into the air, and took Shamir down by the throat. Karissa watched in horror as the panther lashed the man's chest open with a single swipe of his paw.

Shamir's wail gurgled to silence as his feet thrashed the ground and went still. The car at the end of the alley sped away, tires squealing, abandoning the dead men. Then all was quiet, and the cat turned around to confront Karissa.

Her pounding heart lodged in her throat, choking her. Her knees trembled with terror. She met the unblinking gaze of the cat's golden-brown eyes and knew she would be the next to die. But she couldn't move.

As she stood there, frozen with fear, she heard the lid of the garbage dumpster bang open, sending a sharp metallic sound echoing through the night. The cat turned and growled deep in his throat. The rumble vibrated through her, adding to her panic. She peered over her shoulder and saw Josh climbing out of the container.

"Josh, stop!" she cried.

He looked at her but didn't heed the warning. Perhaps he couldn't see the panther in the darkness. Josh slid down the side of the dumpster and dropped to the ground, holding the side of his head where he had been struck. "Jesus!" he declared. "What in the hell happened?"

He walked unsteadily toward her, still holding the side of his head.

"Josh, stop! There's a panther here!"

He lurched to a stop when he caught sight of the shadowy form between him and Karissa. The big cat growled menacingly, lifting one side of its mouth to reveal sharp white teeth as it eased backward, closer to Karissa.

"My God!" Josh whispered. "What do I do?"

"Don't make any sudden moves. It just killed those two men."

Josh glanced at the dead men and then back at the cat. He held up his hands as if to prove he meant no harm and took a step toward Karissa. "Easy, buddy."

The panther growled again, more loudly this time, which convinced Josh to retreat.

"Okay, okay!" Josh sputtered. "I won't come any closer."

"Just stay there, Josh. Don't move. Cats are attracted by movement. Let's see what he does if we just stand still."

Josh stood as stiff as one of her statues, staring down his nose at the cat. The big panther eased back until his long tail brushed against Karissa's shoes. The velvety tip of his tail flicked back and forth across her ankles, as if the cat were making sure she stayed put. She swallowed back a scream.

Minutes passed. Karissa felt a sheen of sweat between her skin and her silk shirt. Still the cat stood guard.

Stood guard.

Was he guarding her? Did he see Josh as a threat? Could the cat be protecting her? Karissa took a few steps backward. The cat paced sideways, positioning himself between her and Josh, but made no move to accost her. Heartened, she stepped backward again. The cat moved with her.

"He thinks he needs to protect me!" she exclaimed, dizzy with relief.

"Crazy animal! So, what do we do?"

"I'm going to try to get to the end of the alley. Just stay where you are, and let's see what he does."

"I wouldn't chance it if I were you. Once you get far enough away from me, he'll probably jump you."

"I don't think so. He would have hurt me by now. I'm going to keep backing up. If you get the chance to make a run for it, Josh, call the police, okay?"

"Sure, but Karissa—"

"I can sense that he isn't a danger to me, Josh. I can't explain how I know. I just do." Karissa gave him a brave smile even though she felt anything but brave inside. "If I get to the road, I'll try to make it to my apartment."

"Okay. Good luck."

Karissa took a few tentative steps down the alley, talking softly to the cat the entire time. The panther snarled but didn't strike out at her. He seemed more intent on keeping his body between Karissa and Josh than impeding her progress.

By the time Karissa reached the main road, her hair lay limp with sweat. She felt the cat's surveillance and was afraid to break into a run or even take a deep breath. Any sudden move and she might become prey, regardless of her brave words to Josh that the cat was no danger.

Perhaps someone driving past would see her and come to her assistance. At nine o'clock at night, however, the chance of rescue was slim. The avenue was deserted. She waved to Josh to assure him that she was still all right, and he waved back. Then she turned and headed for her apartment, praying the panther would not attack her from behind. She looked over her shoulder and saw the dark shadow slink around the corner and pad soundlessly next to her at the base of the linden trees. By the time she reached the stone stairs of her brownstone, she had begun to think of the cat as a shadowy companion instead of a threatening beast.

She fished her keys out of her pocket and slid them in the lock. The panther watched her while his tail flicked back and forth, low to the ground.

"I'm going in now," she declared. "You must go away."

The cat ignored her with regal indifference.

Karissa pushed open the door and stepped into her foyer. She flipped on the lights and looked back at the cat. The panther sat down on the step and lifted its paw. She watched in amazement as the enormous animal began to preen himself. Did the cat intend to stay? She hoped not. She didn't want a mankiller hanging around her front door.

Even though her life had been saved by the cat, she knew she had to alert the animal control center that a dangerous animal was on the loose. The panther had killed two men and couldn't be allowed to roam the streets of Baltimore.

Karissa closed the door and hurried to her phone.

Chapter Two

The police arrived soon after her call. They scoured the neighborhood and returned to her apartment to record her account of the panther attack. They admitted the wounds on the dead men could have been inflicted by the claws and teeth of a big cat. But they couldn't find the animal or any evidence to support her story. Until they finished their investigation, they urged her not to say anything to her neighbors about the supposed panther. Such talk could start a citywide panic. Karissa agreed and watched them go, feeling as if they only half-believed her story.

After the police left Karissa's apartment, and she talked Josh out of spending the night on her couch to protect her, she fell into bed, exhausted. Still, she couldn't sleep. Long past two in the morning she tossed and turned, and in her thrashing, knocked the framed photograph of her paternal grandmother onto the floor.

Bleary with exhaustion, she turned on the lamp and fumbled for the silver frame. She held the photo toward the light to look at the picture she knew by heart. In it her half-Egyptian grandmother, dressed in flapper clothes complete with cloche hat, was listening to a Victrola while smoking on the deck of a ship as it sailed down the Nile.

The photograph represented everything her maternal grandmother hated: the Egyptian blood that was considered a blight on the family tree, a woman smoking or doing anything even remotely unladylike, faddish clothes, and people who defied convention by marrying out of their class. Had Karissa been raised by her Egyptian grandmother Menmet, she might have had a happier childhood. But after the death of her mother, she had been taken in by her blue-blooded Baltimore grandmother. Grandmother Petrie had done her best to eradicate every ounce of defiance and individuality from Karissa through punishment and ridicule.

Karissa sighed and set the silver frame on the nightstand. No matter how much Grandmother Petrie had punished Karissa for her spirited character, she could never obliterate the physical resemblance to her Egyptian grandmother. She had the same black hair and golden skin that had made her grandmother famous. Karissa even had the peculiar birthmark at the base of her skull that her grandmother had been marked with as well. No one ever saw the red splotch, because it was hidden in her hairline, but Karissa often thought of the mark and was secretly pleased to be physically connected to Menmet in that way.

Karissa lay back on her pillow. Now that her marriage was over and Thomas' death was a fading memory, she was ready for something new—not the violence she had suffered that evening, but something like traveling to romantic lands and meeting people from different cultures. She was ready to take over where her grandmother had left off and pursue a life that truly fascinated her. Was that life here in Baltimore at the gallery? More and more she didn't think so.

In the morning, Karissa woke up late, only an hour before the gallery was due to open at ten, hurried through her shower, and skipped her usual morning coffee. Then she threw on a pair of black leggings, a black scoop-necked body shirt, and a new blanket jacket in a planets and stars motif that she had bought to ward off the fall chill. She grabbed her purse, opened the door, and nearly stepped on a pigeon lying on the threshold.

Karissa stared down at the bird and realized it was dead. Poor thing. Perhaps it had died and fallen from the gutter overhead. Karissa looked up at the gutter two stories above. How had a bird managed to fall at an angle so that it landed on her doormat? It didn't seem possible. Perhaps one of the neighbor cats had killed the bird and left it there. Karissa shrugged, went back into the house for some newspaper, and rolled the dead bird inside it. She carried it to the rear of the house and carefully placed it in the garbage can.

Still thinking of the dead bird, she set off down the sidewalk toward the gallery, scanning her surrounds for any signs of the sedan from last night. The police had tried to convince her that the attack was random and perhaps even a case of mistaken identity. But Karissa was convinced that the men had some connection to Mr. Asher.

The autumn morning was overcast and breezy, and leaves scuttled across the walk and over her shoes. Karissa hugged her jacket around her slight frame and increased her pace. At the corner she spied a man in black waiting near a newspaper stand, his hands stuffed in the pockets of his long overcoat. Could it be Mr. Asher?

Alarm mixed with annoyance shot through her. She stepped off the curb to avoid him but noticed he had begun to walk at an angle to intercept her. Karissa looked around frantically, thankful to see a handful of people on the street.

She could call for help if he accosted her. Still, she kept her walk brisk and ignored his approach.

Asher spotted Karissa Spencer at the same instant she caught sight of him If she had been surrounded by a hundred people, he still would have recognized her in the crowd, for she carried herself with a certain aloof pride—a mark of nobility in his day. Karissa was also tall and slender, which lent a fluid litheness to her movements. There was no mistaking her hair either—the luxuriant black veil that hung to her waist. Yesterday he had almost reached out and stroked the shining ebony tresses, and was glad he had controlled himself, because he was quite certain that Karissa Spencer would have taken offense at such a forward gesture. Perhaps she didn't let any man stroke her. The possibility pleased him.

"Miss Spencer!" he called as she gained the other side of the avenue. She acted as if she didn't hear him.

Karissa saw Mr. Asher cross the road, and she increased her pace. Then he leapt from the curb to the sidewalk in an easy spring that she couldn't help but notice out of the corner of her eye. The man was extraordinarily graceful.

"Miss Spencer!"

He strode up to her and matched her pace while he tried to garner her attention. "You should not be walking unescorted."

"I can take care of myself, Mr. Asher." She glared straight ahead. She didn't like persistent people, especially persistent, attractive men. Her husband had been attractive, and she would forever regret the way she had succumbed to him.

Nevertheless, Karissa glanced to the side and let her gaze dart over Mr. Asher.

He wore his hair pulled back and tied at the nape of his neck. Both his ear lobes were pierced but sported no earrings. The collar of a black silk shirt showed beneath his expensive overcoat. Such dark clothing would make most men look sallow and pale, but the black wardrobe only intensified the deep golden tones of Mr. Asher's complexion and highlighted the flash of his teeth and eyes. She couldn't imagine him wearing any other color except for pure white, which would produce the same effect.

Asher returned her glance, and she was struck by the warmth and intelligence in his expression. His golden-brown eyes were bordered by long, dark lashes and attractive laugh lines—definitely not the hard eyes of a criminal. He broke off the glance and looked straight ahead.

"I heard about your trouble last night."

"Oh? How?"

"I saw an account in the morning paper."

"I'm surprised. The attack happened so late."

"True. It never ceases to amaze me how quickly news travels in this day and age, Miss Spencer."

"Or perhaps you know about it because you were there."

Asher stopped. "Do you think I had something to do with the attack?"

"Yes. Those men were Egyptians."

"They have no connection to me."

"I'll bet."

Asher frowned. "They were thugs who work for a man named Mustofa. He is a dangerous man whom, I am afraid, has followed me to your country. And thus, to you."

"Why?"

"Come." He took her elbow before she realized he had even reached for her. "Let us keep walking while I explain. The sooner you get off the street, the better."

"Why? What is this all about!"

"The tomb I mentioned yesterday lies in a place called the Valley of the Damned. In the valley are many other tombs, most of which have probably gone undetected by grave robbers. There is a fortune to be found in the desert, Miss Spencer. Men like Mustofa will do anything to find those tombs, and they don't care whom they torture, kidnap or kill to meet their objective. They are excavating in an area that I believe is very close to the buried sphinx, and if they locate the tombs before I do, the mummy I seek will be lost to me forever."

"But how does this Mustofa character know about me?"

"His spies must have gained access to my files. But I am puzzled by how it could have happened. I have been extremely careful, especially where you are concerned."

She yanked her elbow out of his grip. "You have files on me?"

"Of course." He smiled slightly, showing the lower edge of a line of flawless white teeth. "I have been gathering information for years."

"Why?"

"As I said yesterday, you remain my only key to finding the tomb."

"And will you kidnap and torture me until I agree to help you?"

"My plan to elicit your aid is a nonviolent one, Miss Spencer. But as I said, I shall be persistent."

"You're wasting your time." She strode forward, hoping to outdistance him, but he kept up with her, effortlessly. "A television crew is going to be here next week to start filming a piece on my work. I have a ton of things to get done before then."

"I see." Mr. Asher's tone was heavy with disappointment.

By that time, they had reached the gallery. She drew her keys out of her purse and unlocked the door as Asher stood by and watched her hands. Karissa opened the door, just enough to let herself in and prevent his passage, and then looked back at him. "Now, if you will excuse me, Mr. Asher, I have work to do before the gallery opens."

He raised his glance and leveled it upon hers. Whenever she stared directly into his eyes, she felt as if her self-control slipped a notch. She found it very hard to look away. Even the soft low rumble of his voice was hypnotic.

He put his gloved hand on the woodwork just below eye level. "I have a story to tell you that may change your mind, Miss Spencer."

"I doubt it."

"Nevertheless, allow me to take you to lunch this afternoon, and perhaps what I have to say will help you see this matter in a new light."

Karissa gripped the doorknob, her thoughts in turmoil. She hadn't eaten lunch with a man—other than Josh or a client—for years, and never with a man as mysterious and attractive as Mr. Asher. Not until this moment had she realized what a social recluse she'd become.

"Name the time," he said, "and I will call for you."

"Really, Mr. Asher. I—"

"Grant me an hour. That is all I ask."

She sighed and studied his face for signs of deceit but could see only sincerity. "Well, all right. Come back at two. If I can get away, I'll have lunch with you."

"Excellent!" He smiled again, this time with a slow, sensual slant of his mouth. Karissa could imagine the strength and passion of that mouth and how his lips might feel upon her mouth and neck, and her breasts tightened in a sharp twist of arousal. The sensation amazed her, not only because she was thinking of a man in sexual terms, but because she was responding in such a way to a complete stranger.

When she looked back into his eyes, she saw a knowing glint there, as if he had read her mind. She should have been embarrassed to have a man share her thoughts, but with this man she didn't feel embarrassed at all. In fact, his smoldering gaze only made her breasts ache for him more. Was it the blood of her Egyptian grandmother responding to this dark foreigner, or was it her own female instincts reacting to the presence of a strong, physically beautiful male? Whatever it was, she had the strongest urge to reach up and run her palm across his shining black hair, to stroke him, to kiss him—

"Until two then." He inclined his head again, and for a moment she thought he might ask to kiss her hand. Instead, he turned and walked noiselessly away.

Karissa sighed in relief and shut the door. She locked it with trembling hands. Her attraction for Mr. Asher was illogical and dangerous, and it was best that she stay away from him. Before she took a step, however, she was grabbed from behind, her jacket was pulled halfway off, a hand clamped over her mouth, and something jabbed her upper arm. Within seconds, her world reeled into blackness.

When Karissa awoke, she found herself in a small room with plastered white walls and a peeling blue ceiling. The air in the room was so hot she found it hard to take a breath, and the white cotton shift she was draped in stuck to her in damp folds. Woozy and nauseated, Karissa struggled to sit up from the mat where she had been sleeping on the floor. At the movement, cockroaches scuttled across the tile and up the walls.

"Ew!" Karissa cried in disgust. She jumped to her feet, swaying as she fought for balance. Where was she? She blinked the sleep from her eyes and looked down at the long white nightshirt-like garment. Who had dressed her in an Egyptian *galabia*? And why was it so oppressively hot? She stumbled to the small, barred window and stood on tiptoe to peer out. All she could see was an incredibly blue sky, with no hint of clouds, and the fringe of a palm leaf from a tree nearby.

Karissa lowered herself from the window as dark unease spread over her. There was no sky like the Egyptian sky. And no heat as dry and intense as the heat off the Eastern Desert. Somehow, she must have been transported to the valley of the Nile. She sank against the wall, stunned that she had been kidnapped and taken to a foreign country. But by whom? Mustofa or Mr. Asher?

The answer wasn't long in coming. Soon after she awakened, a thin man with a gun opened the door and ordered her out of the room. She tried to speak to him, but he claimed not to know English. Frustrated, Karissa stumbled through the doorway, still feeling groggy and clumsy. They must have given her a tranquilizer at the gallery and had kept her drugged for days. Rage burned through her. She detested the fact that she had been controlled, especially without her knowledge, and was still a prisoner. She trudged behind the man across a dusty courtyard with a broken fountain. The water feature made her long for something to drink. Her throat was like sandpaper.

She was taken into a yellow house on the other side of the courtyard. Relieved to be out of the heat, but still parched, Karissa followed her guide and was shown into a small parlor off the main hall. A short gaunt man with prominent brown eyes stood near the window, smoking a foul-smelling cigarette. He turned at her entrance and smiled, taking a long drag on the cigarette as he watched Karissa cross the floor toward him. He was balding and had a thin black mustache that traced the line of his full upper lip. His clothes appeared well-made, but his white jacket and trousers were slightly out of date. He wore expensive crocodile shoes but smoked cheap tobacco by the smell of it. The smoke made her feel sick.

"Ah, Miss Spencer," he greeted.

"Mr. Mustofa, I presume?" She was so angry she could barely force out the words.

He smiled as if pleased that she knew his name and nodded as he held his hands up, palms together, in front of his face. Though the gesture was one of respect, it lost considerable effect because of the cigarette poking through two fingers on his right hand.

"Who do you think you are!" she exclaimed. "Drugging me like that and taking me halfway across the world!"

"Had you not resisted so fiercely, I would not have had to resort to such tactics, Miss Spencer."

He stepped to a side table and lifted an earthenware pitcher. With great deliberation he poured a glass of water. "I would expect that you are thirsty, Miss Spencer."

"Yes." She wanted to snatch the glass from his hand, but she stood where she was, unwilling to be manipulated. Mr. Mustofa smiled and took a long appreciative drink. Her entire attention focused upon the sparkling glass and the slow bob of his Adam's apple.

When he finished, he let out a sigh of satisfaction and smiled. "You may have all the water you like, Miss Spencer. And it is bottled water, by the way. But first, you must promise to help me." He set the glass down on a nearby table, and she followed the movement with burning eyes.

"Help you do what?" she croaked through cracked lips.

Mustofa came around the table. "I want you to show me where a certain valley is, one you stumbled upon as a young woman."

"You expect me to help you, after you treat me like this?"

"You have no choice." Mustofa pointed the cigarette at her to emphasize his words. "You are my prisoner, Miss Spencer. And until you show me where the ruins of the lost sphinx are located, you will not have anything to eat or drink. Do you understand?"

"And if I can't remember?"

"I will know you are lying to me, because—" He tapped two fingertips on the side of his balding head. "I have been informed that you have a photographic memory."

"If you think I can remember everything, you're a bigger fool than you look!"

Mustofa's black brows came together in a scowl. Abruptly, he turned.

"Walaal!" he barked.

The door burst open and the thin man with the gun hurried into the room.

"Get this harlot out of my sight. I do not want to see her until morning."

"Yes, Mr. Mustofa." The thin man grabbed Karissa's left arm, but she jerked away.

"Keep your hands off me!" she said, realizing the guard had lied to her about knowing English. He had understood every word Mustofa had said.

"And do not let her talk you into giving her food or water. She will have nothing until she learns better manners."

"Yes, Mr. Mustofa."

"Starving me will get you nowhere," Karissa retorted. "I am worth nothing to you dead."

He turned around, his bony face flushed with anger. "You are worth less if your memory is faulty. So, use the coming hours to think, Miss Spencer. I am sure if you try, you can dredge up some childhood memories."

Karissa swept out of the room, shoulders straight and head held high. She was not about to cooperate with a bully like Mr. Mustofa, even if she could remember the lost sphinx. She would have to find some way of escape.

Asher hailed a taxi at the airport and jumped in the back. Though the car was air-conditioned, Asher felt sweat break out beneath his suit. Already the sun hung low in the sky, which meant he didn't have much time in which to find Karissa Spencer. Because of his worry for the American woman, he had made risky travel arrangements and had prayed the plane would touch down at the Luxor Airport before the sun sank behind the western cliffs. He was also praying that she was being held at Mustofa's compound, because he could probably reach the place before sunset. Still, to Asher, the traffic seemed to crawl through town.

The taxi rolled to a stop in front of a small yellow house bordered by a high wall. Asher dropped a large bill in the driver's hand and slipped out of the cab.

"Keep the change," Asher said, not wanting to take the time to haggle over the fare.

"What about your bags, sir?"

His bags. In his haste, Asher had completely forgotten about the three leather suitcases in the trunk of the taxi. "Take them to this address, will you?" Asher slipped his hand in his pocket and drew out a business card. He dipped into his wallet for another bill. "And here. This should cover it."

"All right."

The taxi pulled away from the cracked sidewalk just as the ringing began in Asher's ears—the first sign that the sun had melted into the horizon. Then all the noises around him roared to life as a more primal, acute sense of hearing kicked in.

In Karissa's prison cell the hours dragged on, interrupted only by the scuttling cockroaches and the call to prayer by the Islamic muezzin at sunset and then again as the shadows of night crept into her small chamber. Cool air off the Nile drifted in through her window, bringing with it the aroma of street vendor food and the sounds of people taking their evening strolls, laughing and talking in the distance, too far away to hear the muffled scream of a woman imprisoned on the outskirts of town. Karissa knew it would be useless to cry out anyway. She would be punished by the guard if she tried anything so foolish. Hopeless and frustrated, she stretched out on the mat and drifted in and out of sleep, feverish with thirst and weak from hunger.

Sometime during the night, Karissa awoke to the sound of voices. Her guard was talking with someone. She sat up and listened, trying to remember the Arab phrases she had learned as a child, but she couldn't make sense of the conversation. Soon, however, she deduced that the thin man was being relieved by a new guard, whose voice was much raspier than the first guard's.

Karissa waited until Walaal left, and then she pounded on the door. "Sir?" she called.

She heard a rustling sound and a metallic clink. "Yes?"

"Please, may I have a drink of water? I am so thirsty."

"Well…"

She heard the lock turn over and stepped back as the door eased open. Standing in the moonlight was a burly man with a grizzled face and a dirty rag wrapped around his head. At the sight of her, he grinned, and his eyes lit up.

"Well, well, well."

Instantly, she regretted her request. The guard took a step toward her, but she held her ground, even though she wanted to stay far away from him.

"A drink, eh?" he chuckled. "That could be arranged, my little lotus blossom—for a price."

"I have no money."

"I am willing to barter. That's the way we do things here in Luxor." His grin widened, displaying teeth stained by nicotine.

Karissa blinked back her disgust. She calculated the distance between his large body and the open door. If she could entice him further into the chamber and switch places with him, she might be able to escape. But did she have the strength to run?

Still, this might be her only chance to get away from Mustofa. She brushed back a strand of hair and lowered her voice to a more seductive level. "What did you care to exchange?"

"What do you think?" The guard's eyebrows raised in delight as he ambled forward. "A taste of you for a taste of water."

She ducked away and turned playfully, so that her back was to the door, and he was no longer between her and the outside world. He chuckled, obviously enjoying the game.

"First, my drink."

"Oh, you are hard ones, you American girls."

She nodded and kept her distance as he chuckled and went back outside. He returned with an old plastic bleach container. The thought of putting her lips on the discolored rim of the bottle nearly made her retch, but thirst overrode her disgust.

"There you go, my flower." The guard held out the bottle.

She tipped it to her lips and let the tepid water fill her parched mouth. In great gulps she drank, forgetting to take it easy, until the guard pulled away the bottle, laughing.

"Do not drink too much! You will be sick." He capped the bottle. "I do not want you puking all over me when I am..." He made a lewd thrust with his hips. Karissa wiped her mouth with the back of her hand and watched him. He leaned over to set the bottle on the floor and reached for his gun to lay it on the tile as well, and at that moment Karissa lunged for the door.

The water and fear gave her the strength to run. She dashed through the door and across the courtyard, hunting for a gate in the high wall that surrounded the compound. The guard pounded behind her. Within seconds, Karissa knew her starved body was quickly losing power and she would never outdistance him. Frantically she ran along the base of the wall, praying she wouldn't step on a scorpion or snake in the darkness.

The guard grabbed her from behind. She tumbled to the sandy ground on hands and knees. The guard pushed her hard in the small of her back, shoving her face down in the dirt, and then he pinned her rump and thighs with one knee.

"Get off me, you lout!"

"You are going to like this." He chuckled and fumbled with his pants. "American men are sissies. But we Egyptians are men. Real men."

He grabbed her elbow, lifted his leg from her rump, and wrenched her onto her back. He grinned. "We take what we want, and our women love it!"

"Like hell!" Karissa glared at him and kicked wildly, trying to hurt him.

He only laughed and clamped a dirty hand over her mouth. She pummeled him with her fists, but her blows seemed to have no effect on him. He reached for the hem of her *galabia* and yanked it up her thighs. Karissa froze, outraged that she was about to be violated by this stranger. Then he fumbled at her panties while Karissa writhed, using the last bit of her strength to fight him off.

She glared at his sickening mouth and thrashed her head back and forth to avoid his kiss. His eyes gleamed in the darkness. She felt a wave of light-headedness overtake her but refused to give in to it. She couldn't faint now. She couldn't surrender to this disgusting man.

Suddenly a menacing growl rolled out of the shadows. The guard grunted in surprise and raised his head.

The growl came again, louder this time.

"Who is there!" the guard demanded.

A dark shape materialized from behind a clump of palms, and with measured footfalls, a large, black cat came toward them. The panther was in no hurry, as if he were certain his prey was incapable of escape. He padded closer, his shoulder blades flowing up and down like the well-oiled pistons of a killing machine, and his eyes uncompromisingly cold.

"Lord Azhur!" the guard gasped. He scrambled out from between Karissa's legs, reached for his pants, and lumbered to his feet. "Please, Lord—"

The panther bunched his muscles and leapt upward.

Chapter Three

Karissa scrambled to her feet as the big cat lunged upon the guard. It looked like the same black panther that had saved her life in Baltimore. If so, how had the cat traveled to Egypt from the United States? Perhaps it wasn't a real cat at all. Perhaps none of this was real. She half-expected to wake up from a nightmare and find herself in her house in The States.

Yet the scrapes on her knees and the sand in her hair were very real, as was the body being dragged into the clump of palms near the wall. Karissa turned away in disgust at the sight of the guard's limp legs bumping along the sand as the panther pulled his victim into the shadows. She didn't condone killing, but she was grateful to have escaped being raped by the guard.

Where would she go now, though?

Her first concern was getting out of the compound. Karissa glanced up at the high wall that rose three feet above her head. She would never be able to scale it. She would have to find a gate. Fighting a ringing in her ears and the shakiness in her legs, she stumbled forward.

Within moments, she felt a presence behind her and glanced backward to see the panther loping toward her. Instead of walking alongside her as he had done in Baltimore, the panther padded ahead and guided her to a small portal. Karissa opened the wooden door and stepped into a lane that led to a littered alley bordered by tall apartments and shops strung together with clotheslines and electrical wires. She paused, having no idea what to do or which way to go, especially in the middle of the night with no money and no identification. The cat seemed to have an agenda of his own, however, and kept walking. After a moment, he paused to look back at her. He blinked, and his tail flicked back and forth as if he waited for her to catch up.

Karissa decided to follow his lead. After all, the cat had saved her life on two occasions. She walked after him as he loped through the quiet Luxor streets, past sleepy homes, darkened apartment houses, closed bazaars, and ghostly mosques. Karissa struggled to keep up with him. Other than following the cat, she had no alternative but to throw herself on the mercy of the U.S. Embassy, which she decided to do in the morning, should the panther lead her astray.

The city stretched endlessly along the river. Soon her steps were dragging, as she suffered from thirst and hunger. She had used her reserves to fight off the guard, and now she operated purely on determination and pride. But how many more steps could she force herself to take?

As if the cat read her mind, he led her to a shadowed alcove and sat on his haunches, waiting for her to catch up. Karissa could hear the musical tinkle of water and her spirits rose. The panther had led her to a small fountain attached to the side of a building. She could see the stream of water glinting in the moonlight. Karissa almost cried out in gratitude as she thrust her hands into the water and cupped mouthful after mouthful to her lips.

Her mother's frequent warning to drink only bottled water ran through her thoughts, but in her desperation, Karissa ignored the voice and chanced illness. Besides, she had drunk water out of the dirty bleach bottle, and that was worse.

Feeling much better after quenching her thirst, Karissa trailed after the cat. Soon the panther turned down a tree-lined street that took them south of town. The city became a sprawl with the houses farther apart. Here and there an irrigated field bordered the road. The cat veered to the right and padded down a smaller lane that wound through trees bordering the Nile, which gleamed in the distance. Karissa stumbled after him, sure that she would last only a few more minutes. She had never felt so weak or hungry.

They passed between two pillars and continued down an avenue toward a two-story house surrounded by the graceful trunks and drooping fronds of date palms. She followed the panther to the front of the house, up the wide granite steps and onto the veranda. The cat took her to the front door and then sat down.

Karissa glanced at the panther. "Now what?" she asked, unsure why they were at this residence. Did he expect her to knock on the door?

Before Karissa could decide what to do, she felt a swirling sensation in her head and her vision sparkled and tipped. Her body had reached its physical limit. She staggered sideways and crumpled to the cool granite slabs of the porch.

When she woke up, she was lying in a clean bed draped in a festoon of mosquito netting. Startled to be in unfamiliar surroundings, Karissa lurched to a sitting position and glanced around. She was in a large white room tastefully decorated in brass and wood and potted plants. A half-empty glass of water stood on the bedside table.

She couldn't remember getting into the bed, much less drinking the water. Had someone helped her do both things? Rays of morning sunlight slanted through the open doors of the balcony and poured across the blue Persian carpet. She must have been sleeping for hours.

Karissa slipped out of the bed and teetered for a moment, light-headed with hunger, and caught a glimpse of something white just beyond the French doors of the balcony. Holding her head, she walked across the thick carpet and looked down to see a dead ibis on the pale tile. She turned away in dismay that another dead creature had been left on her doorstep. But her hunger and curiosity concerning her whereabouts soon overtook all thought of the ibis. She needed food and hoped the master who ruled this house would be more accommodating than Mr. Mustofa.

Before she could decide whether or not to crawl back into bed, she heard a light rap on the bedroom door.

"Miss Spencer?" A lightly accented female voice spoke from the other side.

"Yes?"

"Would you like some breakfast?"

Would she? Her salivary glands leaped into action at the mere mention of food.

"Yes." She hurried to open the door. In the hall stood a small pudgy woman with black hair plaited in a braid that hung to her hips. She was probably in her fifties and had large dark brown eyes that glistened with kindness. But what caught Karissa's attention and held it, was the tray of food the woman carried into the room.

"I am Eisha, the housekeeper, Miss Spencer."

"You know who I am?"

Eisha nodded and swept across the room to a small table.

"My master has told me of you."

"Your master? And who might he be?"

"My master wishes to tell you all himself. But he does not rise until midday. While you wait, you must eat and bathe and rest."

Karissa didn't appreciate the mystery surrounding her host and didn't admire a man who slept late, but she kept her views to herself. For now, she would take advantage of his hospitality, if only to fortify herself for another escape. She stared at the plates of food Eisha uncovered: cold meats, pickles, savory foul beans and bread, and a mound of steaming, scrambled eggs. Out of a silver coffee carafe drifted the wonderful aroma of strong Egyptian coffee, flavored with cloves. The smell nearly made her swoon.

"I am not accustomed to serving American breakfasts," Eisha said, setting a place on the table. "Is this satisfactory?"

"It looks wonderful!" Karissa smiled shakily. "Thank you."

Eisha straightened. "When you are done, just ring the little bell." She gestured to a brass bell on the tray. "I will prepare a nice bath for you."

"Thank you." She pulled off a piece of bread and consumed it without chewing it more than three times. Next came a pickle and a forkful of egg. While Karissa ate, Eisha poured her a cup of coffee. Karissa tried the spicy beans and washed them down with a long sip of the fragrant coffee. In moments she felt the empowering effect of the food. She turned to the housekeeper.

"Eisha, I need to get back to the United States. Is there a phone somewhere that I could use?"

"Yes. But eat first and then you may make your arrangements. I am sure my master wants you to stay until he has a chance to speak with you."

Karissa wasn't sure if she had exchanged her miserably hot cell in the middle of Luxor for a more extravagant one. But she decided to finish the meal first and ask questions later.

At half-past noon, Karissa walked down the hall toward the garden, where the master of the house awaited. Eisha had helped her arrange for money to be wired to a hotel in Luxor. Then Karissa had phoned Josh to tell him where she was and give him the phone number and address of the house in which she was staying. But Josh wasn't at home or at the gallery, and she was forced to leave a message on the answering machine. When she was done, she decided to wait for the master of the house to stir before she thanked him and went on her way.

Since her Western clothes had been stripped away by Mustofa, Karissa had been given a linen dress by Eisha to replace the dirty *galabia*. The garment was fashioned of the finest gossamer and was more feminine than anything she had ever worn. The wrap was pleated in a way that concealed her intimate areas while at the same time afforded the barest covering in the heat. Instead of feeling awkward in the foreign attire, Karissa experienced a strange sensation of deja vu, as if she had worn such a dress before, when she knew very well that she had not.

She walked toward the door that opened onto the garden. Near the door was a cage filled with chattering finches. A few steps beyond was another cage that contained two falcons.

More cages were scattered throughout the garden, all housing birds native to Egypt, from hoopoe birds to swallows. Karissa's heart went out to the creatures. Though they lived in a beautiful garden and were obviously well cared for, they were still prisoners, just as she was.

In the garden beyond, she could barely make out the figure of a dark-haired man through the shifting fronds of the palms. He was dressed in a white loose-fitting shirt, the sleeves rolled up on his forearms, and a pair of white pants that hung from his lean hips. While she watched him, he fed pieces of fruit to a scarlet parrot perched on his wrist. She could tell that the man spoke to the bird by the way the creature cocked its head from side to side and stared at him.

Karissa stepped toward the man, intending to offer her thanks and then leave for the hotel in Luxor where she had sent funds.

Asher heard a light step behind him, turned around, and was struck speechless by the sight of Karissa Spencer in the linen gown. She walked toward him, and he was lost. All he could see was the woman he had loved thousands of years ago. Senefret. Through the branches of the sycamore-fig trees came a mirage from his past—a tall, fine-boned, exquisitely beautiful woman dressed in purest white. He stared as his heart leapt in his chest. Ah, beautiful Senefret! She was even more lovely than his memory of her.

For a long moment he let himself succumb to the vision and slipped into the past where he had loved a woman with all his heart. But as Karissa drew closer, he pushed the vision from his thoughts. It was unfair to himself and to Karissa to invest the American woman with the traits and history of an Egyptian beauty long since dead.

Long since dead but not forgotten, Asher's heart reminded him. Until that moment he had been able to ignore the anguish buried inside him. But one look at Karissa and the heartache roared up like a wall of flame. The pain in his chest threatened to send him to his knees.

When Karissa drew closer and recognized him, her expression changed from open interest to dark suspicion, and the mirage vanished.

"Mr. Asher!" she exclaimed in disgust, stopping at the fountain a few feet away. "I should have known."

"Miss Spencer," he replied, ignoring her angry remark. "Good afternoon." His tongue tripped over the English words that never came naturally to him, no matter how many years he spoke the choppy language. He put the parrot on a roost.

Karissa's scowl deepened, shadowing her luminous dark brown eyes and wrinkling the flesh above her delicate, pointed nose. He had the wildest urge to press his lips to the wrinkle and smooth it with a kiss but knew such a gesture would infuriate her.

"You had this planned all along," she continued, stepping forward in anger. "The thugs, the kidnapping, the rescue by your trained panther—"

"Trained panther?"

"Yes. The cat that kills people and leaves gifts at my doorstep. You could be arrested for manslaughter, you know, owning a dangerous pet like that."

"I have no such pet, Miss Spencer, I assure you."

"Then what brought me here last night?"

"Whatever it was, it was no pet."

"It seemed to know where you live."

He shrugged off the insinuation and smiled, mesmerized by the soft sloping curve between her nose and lip. Her mouth moved enticingly whenever she spoke, drawing down the tip of her nose. He wanted to touch that nose with his, to feel her lips upon his skin, to discover the taste of her neck. His loins stirred, almost painfully. In the sixteen years he had been in Luxor, he had never encountered a woman who could make his blood race like this one. He forced himself to look away.

"Are you rested?" he asked, changing the subject. "Did you get enough to eat?"

"Yes, but don't think you can buy my cooperation with the bed and breakfast routine. I appreciate the hospitality, Mr. Asher, but I plan to leave. Tonight."

He sighed. "Even so, can I not interest you in lunch? You agreed to meet me for lunch in Baltimore and to hear what I have to say. Will you not honor that agreement here in Luxor?"

"Why? It's useless." She swept away from him, turning her back.

"Useless? In what way?" Asher's gaze traveled down the shapely curves of her hips and legs as he imagined how it would feel to press against her slender length. His loins quickened again, and he breathed in sharply.

"Nothing you say could bring back my memory. Half a dozen doctors have done everything they know to induce me to remember. But I just can't."

"Can't or won't, Miss Spencer?"

She turned to face him, and her expression was as cold as marble. "What are you implying?"

"That you don't want to face the truth. That there is something about the sphinx that you don't want to remember."

"Well, it's easy to see why, isn't it? My mother died from the curse of the sphinx and my father vanished off the face of the earth."

"Oh?" Asher crossed his arms and tilted his head. "Did your father really disappear, Miss Spencer?"

He studied her face, searching for the truth in her reaction. She stared at him, her eyes wide. For an instant a tense silence hung between them, and then she whirled around and marched to the fountain. Asher rushed after her, determined to help her remember. He would have reached up for her bare shoulders, but she turned and glared at him.

"Leave me alone, Mr. Asher."

"I only want to help you."

"So, I can help you find the sphinx. What a noble motive, sir." Full of disdain, she presented her back to him again.

"I may be the only one who can help you remember, Miss Spencer."

"And why are you so special?"

"Because." He leaned forward, closed his eyes, and breathed in the perfume of her hair. Every particle in his body wanted to reach for the woman standing so tantalizingly nearby. "I was there that night."

He saw her entire body go rigid.

"Yes," he went on, "I was there. And I think I can guess what happened to your father."

"You are wrong," she replied in a thick tone. "No one else was there. Just me and then later my mother."

"Perhaps you were not aware that I was there."

"No!" Karissa shook her head vehemently. "I saw nothing! No one! It was the middle of the desert. I would have noticed."

"Some things are not what they appear to be, especially when seen through the eyes of a child."

"I wasn't a child. I was twelve years old."

"A child, nevertheless." He softened his tone. "You were a little girl who saw something she could not fit into the definitions of her world. And so, she chose not to define it or examine it, ever again."

"I don't know what you're talking about," she retorted, taking a step toward the house.

He realized she was about to bolt away and grabbed a wrist to stop her.

"Let me go!" she shouted.

"Not until you look at the truth. You know what happened at the sphinx, Miss Spencer. Admit it to yourself. Take back that missing part of your life."

"No!" She yanked her arm, but he held on tightly.

His heart ached to see the pain in her eyes, but he pressed on, determined to finish what he had begun. "You saw something that you simply cannot face."

"No!"

"Yes, Miss Spencer."

She shook her head and then covered her face with her free hand. Wrenching sobs heaved in her chest, and she hunched over, miserable. Was the truth finally reaching her?

"You have it all wrong."

"How was it, then?" he inquired gently. "Tell me."

"I can't. I can't!" Tears streamed down her cheeks. He released her wrist, and she covered her face with both hands as if ashamed to be seen crying. She curled away from him, her white shift billowing around her sandals.

An overwhelming surge of compassion washed over Asher. He couldn't let her stand there alone, suffering. He reached out and surrounded her in a gentle embrace and tucked her against his chest until her tears subsided. To his amazement, she let herself be drawn to him. Asher eased his fingers into the thick mass of her raven hair and urged her to lean her head against his chest while he slowly stroked her back. His body sang to her surrender when she placed her small palms on his torso and let her weight sway into him. He breathed in her scent and slowly increased the pressure of his embrace. He couldn't help himself. Though his aim was to offer her comfort, he couldn't deny his need for her.

Isis, how he longed to kiss her. He lowered his head and brushed the tip of his nose across the hair at her temple. At the movement, she turned her head, and his jaw grazed her cheek. Asher's breath caught in his throat as her smooth skin passed over his. For a heart-thudding instant, she allowed her cheek to linger against his, and a tiny sigh escaped her lips.

"Karissa!" he said, his voice rough with passion. He pulled back to look at her—at her smooth, golden skin, her regal nose, and her luminous, almost black, eyes. She needed no line of kohl to accentuate the almond sweep of her lashes. Her eyes were arresting, even when dotted by tears, even when filled with anguish.

Slowly, oh so slowly, she raised her head. Tears hung from the ends of her sooty lashes. Her lips parted at the center of her mouth. She let out a soft sigh, almost of wonder, as if one of his finches flew around her and then upward, winging her heartache into the sky.

Something ephemeral shifted between their bodies and spirits.

For a moment he stared down at her. He had no wish to denigrate her grief by initiating intimate physical contact between them. He had no intention of forcing himself on a woman who wasn't interested in his attentions. But for an instant he saw the light of desire flicker through her glance and knew that he had not misinterpreted her sigh.

With a low moan born of loneliness and hunger, he gathered her into his arms and bent to her tear-streaked face.

Chapter Four

The kiss began as a gentle press of Asher's lips upon hers, but once he tasted the lushness of her mouth, he couldn't hold back. Karissa's lips were like a perfectly ripe plum—dark, luscious, soft and wonderfully sweet. As he pulled her even closer, he heard her sigh again. The wistful sound set him on fire. Asher pushed his hand into her hair, reveling in the way the silky strands slipped between his fingers.

The women he had known in the ancient days had worn ornate braided wigs, perfumed by cones made of animal fat placed on the tops of their heads. A man could not caress such coifs with the freedom afforded by Karissa's natural, luxuriant hair. He cradled her head with his palm as she leaned back to accept him. Then he slanted an intense kiss upon her, using his tongue to stroke the line between her lips until she allowed him entrance to her warm mouth. She opened to him.

It was Asher's turn to sigh this time, and the raggedness of the sound shocked him. What kind of hold did the American woman have on him, that he was eager to give himself to her already? Yet he wanted her more than he had ever wanted a woman, even more than—

Asher broke off the thought and slipped his tongue into Karissa's mouth. He felt her exploring him, tentatively at first and then with a boldness that inflamed him. The kiss grew harder, hotter, wilder. Karissa's hands released their grip on his white cotton shirt and slid up his torso. She curved her arms around his neck and hugged him fiercely, grinding against his mouth as if she had hungered for him for thousands of years. Her passion took him by surprise. And yet, one night long ago, Senefret had reacted to his kiss in just this way.

Karissa's breasts pressed against his chest, and he could feel the hard buds of her nipples. The thought that she was already aroused made him grow as hard as granite. He closed his eyes as the line blurred between this woman and the woman from his past, and he let his body surge to life for the first time in over a decade. Then he slipped his hands down the graceful slope of her back and cupped her rump, pulling her against him and leaving no doubt as to his desire for her. She pressed into him, perfectly formed to fit against him, which only made him ache for her more. Karissa sighed at his ear, driving him mad with her sweet, warm breath, until he couldn't resist lifting her up slightly, just enough to ease her over his burgeoning flesh. He sucked in a long and tortured breath and fought the urge to make love to her here in the garden. He had no right to ask that of her. Truth be told, he had no right to kiss her and hold her like this.

Sighing, Asher let her slide back to the ground. He pulled away from her mouth and gazed down at her, surprised that he had reacted so strongly to her. After a moment, she released his neck and let her hands flow down the front of his shirt as she glanced up to meet his gaze. The plum of her mouth looked delightfully crushed.

Off in the distance someone called to him, but the summons barely registered. Asher drew his hands away from her back and lightly grasped her elbows, denying himself the pleasure of kissing her again. If he tasted her mouth once more, he knew he would find it impossible to let her go.

"Are you all right now?" he asked lowly, not sure whether he referred to her emotional outburst—which seemed to have occurred hours ago—or to the passion that had just flared between them.

Karissa nodded and blushed, and then stepped away from him. "Isn't that Eisha calling you, Mr. Asher?" she asked in an endearingly uneven voice.

Asher glanced at the garden entrance where his housekeeper stood, holding a tray of food, and then returned his attention to Karissa. He ran the pad of his thumb along her cheekbone in a gentle caress.

"To you my name is Asheris." He put the accent on the middle syllable, which made a sound like the wind in the desert.

"A-share-iss." She let the name whisper through her teeth.

He smiled quietly, pleased to hear his real name on her lips. "Come," he said, guiding her forward with a light touch on her lower back. "Take the midday meal with me so that we may talk at last."

Karissa strolled beside him to a secluded table near the fountain. There she spent the late luncheon in a strange state of disquiet, worried that by kissing Mr. Asher—Asheris—she had lost her objectivity in regard to him. She was also concerned that he would bring up the lost sphinx again, and she refused to think about it. He had taken her dangerously close to the edge of remembrance, and she wasn't ready to step into the abyss beyond. Compounding her disquiet was the physical and mental distraction produced by the man sitting across the table from her. She could not afford to waste any time gawking at him. She intended to listen to his story and get back to Baltimore.

Karissa ate sparingly, too keyed up to be hungry for food. As she nibbled, she couldn't help but recall the passion she had just experienced in Asheris' arms. But how serious could a man be about a woman he had known for a mere few hours? She had learned to be wary of men who displayed deep passion for no apparent reason and had vowed never to fall for a charmer again. It seemed to be a family weakness to succumb to handsome men, and she was determined to break the chain.

She unleashed pomegranate seeds from their husk as she analyzed her feelings for the graceful, elegant Egyptian across from her. There was more than shallow attraction for him in her heart, so much more that she experienced a sudden swell of tenderness whenever she glanced at him. The undeniable attraction was intensified by a curious feeling of familiarity—that she already knew Asheris as an old friend, that she was accustomed to the width of his shoulders, the intelligent tilt of his head, and the slow, sensual slant of his smile.

She chided herself for thinking she already knew him. Such thoughts were for foolish romantics who believed in love at first sight, soulmates and previous lives. Utter nonsense.

As if Asher could read her thoughts, he looked up from his plate and gazed at her without speaking, his eyes full of warmth. She returned the gaze, wondering why she wasn't nervous when staring at a man for minutes on end. She had never understood the words "falling into someone's eyes", but now she knew precisely what the phrase meant. She felt her spirit plunge into Asheris' soul and had no power to hold herself back.

"I am supposed to be convincing you to help me," he declared at last, tearing apart a piece of flat bread and giving half to her.

She accepted it. "Yes. You mentioned something about a story."

"Indeed." His smile faded as he tore off a bite-sized piece and chewed it slowly. For a long moment he stared at the line of acacia trees in his garden, but she could tell that his eyes weren't seeing the trees at all. He was contemplating the telling of his tale and searching for the right words. Judging by the look in his eyes, the story was not a happy one. Perhaps nothing connected to the lost sphinx was pleasant.

"Is it a true story?" she asked.

"Yes. From long ago." He set down the bread. "It concerns my—ancestors."

The pause made her wonder if the story was connected to something or someone much closer than Asheris' ancestors. But she said nothing and waited for him to begin.

He sighed and raised his incredible glowing eyes to meet hers. "A long time ago there was a beautiful priestess named Senefret. She had been raised by the worshippers of Sekhmet, the lion goddess, to become the Great Royal Wife of the pharaoh, but she did not want to wed the pharaoh. He was a cruel, misshapen man given to bouts of insanity, which I have learned from modern science, was probably the result of intermarriage. You know, do you not, that pharaohs often wedded their sisters?"

"Yes, I've heard that."

"Unfortunately, the practice weakened the bloodline. So it was for the pharaoh. And Senefret did not want to spend her life married to such a monster, even though it would bring her glory and wealth."

"To some people, glory and wealth don't mean all that much," Karissa noted, thinking of Grandmother Petrie and her rich but sterile life. She wanted nothing of that world.

"Agreed." Asheris chewed another bite of bread and went on. "So, Senefret decided to take her fate into her own hands. She was a brave woman with a bold spirit, and she decided to run off to the northeastern border where her older brother, who was a general in the Egyptian army, was fighting nomadic invaders. She was certain her brother would help her escape her marriage. But when she got to the border, she found her brother suffering from a mortal wound. He died in her arms.

Grief-stricken and knowing she had lost her only supporter, Senefret decided to die fighting. The following morning, she donned her brother's battle gear and rode to war next to the commander-in-chief of the army, who was half-brother to the pharaoh and a great favorite of the people. During the course of the battle, she saved the commander-in-chief's life, and in turn, he snatched her out of danger just as she was about to receive a fatal arrow. They rode back to camp in the commander's chariot.

A bath was drawn and wine poured, and the commander insisted that the young general join him in a toast while he bathed. The commander stripped, unknowingly revealing his well-hewn soldier's body to the virginal priestess. Instead of turning away, Senefret decided to find out what it would be like to have a real man before she died in battle or was shipped back to Thebes. She removed her male attire and offered herself to him.

The commander did not know who she was or where she had come from, and she refused to tell him. She asked that he kiss her, not question her, and the commander willingly granted her request, for she was a beautiful woman and her bravery on the field had mightily impressed him. For an entire night they made love. Then, before the camp awakened, Senefret slipped out of his bed to return to her brother's tent. On the way she was captured by an agent of the Temple of Sekhmet, who had sent a spy to follow her."

Karissa stared at him, mesmerized by the story and completely forgetting about the pomegranate on her plate. The tale seemed so familiar to her. Had her father told her the story long ago when he tucked her into bed?

"So, then what happened?" Karissa asked.

"Senefret was dragged back to Thebes. There it was discovered that she had been deflowered and was no longer fit for the pharaoh. This was an abomination to the gods. She was executed and entombed in the Valley of the Damned, forever barred from entering the Afterworld."

"That's horrible!"

"Yes. And Senefret's body," he paused, and for a moment he seemed to have difficulty in speaking, "Her body is the one I must recover and re-inter, so that she may find peace in the Fields of Iaru where she belongs."

"Fields of Iaru?"

"The equivalent of your heaven."

Karissa studied Asheris' face. While telling the tale of Senefret, he had expressed genuine emotion. Either he was a good actor, or he was personally connected to the characters in the story.

"How does this story pertain to your—ancestors?" she inquired.

"My family is related to the commander in the story."

"Oh." She felt let down by the easy explanation.

"But there is more to tell of the commander." Asheris poured a glass of wine and offered it to her. "The story is not yet finished."

"Please continue, then." She took the glass and savored the brush of his warm fingers against hers. "Thank you."

"My pleasure." He poured a goblet for himself and slowly took a sip. "As to the commander, after just one night, he knew he had fallen in love with the mysterious Senefret. But he was caught up in his dreams of personal glory and bound by duty to finish the campaign in the north before he pursued a woman and declared his feelings. Half a year later, the commander returned to Thebes as a war hero.

When the commander made inquiries about Senefret, it was discovered that he was the man responsible for deflowering the priestess meant for the pharaoh. The High Priestess of the Temple of Sekhmet accused him of the crime and threw him in prison. In those days the priests and priestesses were very powerful, almost as powerful as the pharaoh himself. When they demanded the life of a mortal, they usually got it, especially if that mortal had offended the king or committed a sin. The commander's fate was sealed. On the day of his death, he was told what happened to his beloved. He was devastated. Then, for that single night with Senefret, the commander was forced to forfeit his life—but not, I might add, in a conventional way."

"What did they do to him?"

"They mummified him alive."

Karissa froze in disbelief, the wine goblet pressed against her lip. She lowered the glass. "They what?"

"They mummified him alive. It was a practice known to them, a secret now lost."

"Mummified alive? What does that mean? How?"

Asheris took a long draught of wine. "I do not know precisely. Many of the secret rites have been lost over the centuries. But the fact remains that the commander was buried alive and cursed by the Temple of Sekhmet to be a living mummy until released by a woman who loved him. The priestesses were certain the curse would imprison him forever, because they knew the only woman who loved the commander was Senefret, and she was already dead."

He heaved a sigh and pressed on, his eyes dark and troubled. "And because the commander was still alive in his tomb, his spirit or *ka* could never leave the earth and travel to the Underworld where it belonged. The Lioness cult therefore damned him to eternal hell, just as they had damned Senefret."

Karissa reached out and slipped her hand over Asheris' right wrist in a gesture of compassion. "This story is very sad."

"Yes." Asheris nodded and covered her hand with his left. "But Osiris, the God of the Underworld, took pity on the lovers. He knew what it was like to be forever damned to remain in one world. So, he lifted the curse, as much as it was in his power to do so. Since he was Lord of the Underworld and Ruler of the Night, he released the commander's *ka* by allowing it to wander free, but only during the night hours. And only in the form of a cat."

"A cat?" Karissa felt a shiver race down her back. "A panther?"

Asheris nodded and silently regarded her as if waiting for her to make additional connections.

"Not the panther I saw at the lost sphinx."

He raised his eyebrows as if to encourage her to reconsider.

"But the panther would have to be thousands of years old! How could he live that long?"

"He is no ordinary beast." He squeezed her hand and then reached for his wine. "He is the spirit of a damned man."

Karissa sat back, trying to take in all that he had said, and fingered the stem of her glass. If what Asheris said was true, she had been saved twice by a mythical panther. If the cat were supernatural, its unearthliness would certainly explain how it had traveled from Baltimore to Luxor. She glanced at her lunch companion.

"So, the panther spirit was the cat who saved my life?"

"Quite likely."

"But why? Why me?"

"Because you are very important to him."

"Because I know the location of the lost sphinx? What has that to do with the mummified commander and the panther?"

"The man was locked inside the sphinx, Karissa. You let him out."

She paled. "When the sphinx collapsed?"

"Yes." Asheris finished his wine. "The sphinx guarded the entrance of the Valley of the Damned. But as everyone knows, the Valley of the Damned is in a barren desert that is constantly altered by wind and sand. No one knows for sure where the ruined sphinx lies buried. No one but you, Karissa. You are the single living soul who holds the key to finding Senefret's body."

"But I can't remember."

"I think you can." He reached for her hand again and surrounded it with the warmth of his palm and fingers. "If you are willing to relive that night, Karissa, to face whatever troubles you about it, you could redeem the soul of a woman whose only sin was to choose personal freedom."

"I can't," Karissa replied in a low voice. She couldn't bear to think of two people trapped forever because of her. Yet the pain of examining the night at the sphinx would be even more acute, much closer to her heart and personal history. Besides, she had no time to get caught up in Asher's fantasy. She had her own problems and her own schedule to consider. She jumped to her feet, knocking back the chair. "I can't. I simply can't help you."

In contrast, he rose to his feet with elegant gracefulness. "But will you not at least try?" he asked softly.

She stared at him, wanting to run far away from him and into his arms at the same time. Was she losing her mind?

He placed his napkin on the table. "Will you at least agree to drive out to the desert with me and take a look? I will make it worth your while."

Karissa raised her chin and studied him. Money would enable her to buy out Josh and break away from his disruptive presence. That in itself would give her a considerable amount of peace of mind, perhaps enough to make up for the craziness of arriving in Baltimore a day or two behind schedule.

"How much money are you willing to pay me if I decide to go with you?" she asked after a long pause.

"One hundred thousand in U.S. funds, plus expenses."

The sum staggered her, but she didn't show her surprise. "I already made a plane reservation for eight o'clock this evening, though."

"I will buy a new ticket for you."

She swept back her hair and noticed that his eyes followed the movement. For a hundred thousand dollars, she could be persuaded to spend one more day in Egypt. "All right, then, Mr. Asher. Let's go."

Chapter Five

Asheris drove his Land Rover through the outskirts of Luxor, dodging trucks piled with grain, schools of bicycles and overloaded buses piled with people and chickens. The chaos and noise didn't seem to faze him. Karissa wondered if Asheris did everything with quiet competence. She glanced at him, appreciating the way he looked in his dark glasses with his hair pulled back to the nape of his neck. Her gaze traveled across his sharp jawline accentuated by the white collar of his shirt and down his arms where the rolled-up sleeves revealed his tanned forearms. She liked the way fine black hair lightly shaded his sinewy arms and could imagine his chest was similarly shadowed.

Asheris shifted into a lower gear and swerved around three camels while Karissa's gaze dropped to his lean thighs draped in a pair of khaki pants. He had long, well-formed legs and narrow aristocratic feet that manipulated the pedals with authority. She could imagine that Asheris always conducted himself with authority. A vision of him moving over her in bed—making love to her with a maddening amount of mastery—flashed through her thoughts. Where had that vision come from?

She flushed and stared out the window, intending to get her mind off the image of Asheris in bed by concentrating on the scenery. Soon, her thoughts raced far ahead of the vehicle, taking everything in, from the wide cobalt-blue river to its much lighter sister sky. Her heart rose with an ache that surprised her. She rolled down the window and sucked in the smell she loved above all others—the languid, brimming-with-life fecundity of the Nile River.

Karissa had been in Egypt for only a few days and was already falling in love again with the lush green valley and the stark golden cliffs that bordered the Nile. She loved the contrasts of Egypt, a place where skyscrapers rose beside pyramids, where cruise ships sailed past feluccas used by fisherman since ancient times, where camel caravans loitered in the parking lots of gas stations. The delightful mixture of the sights and sounds of her childhood came rushing back, filling her heart with a joy so sharp that she sighed out loud.

"What is wrong?" Asheris shot a sidelong glance at her. Sunlight caught his glasses and flashed over the lenses.

"Nothing." She smiled. "It's just good to be back, that's all. I didn't realize how much I missed this place."

She looked at him and saw the corner of his mouth rise in that slow lop-sided smile of his. The sight made her heart do a crazy flip-flop. What was it about this man that could make her react so strongly, just to his smile? Whatever it was, she was in danger of falling under the spell of Egypt again, but in a new, alarming way.

Within forty-five minutes they had climbed through a steep pass in the cliffs and wound up an arid canyon until they reached the desert above. A blast of gritty wind blindsided them at the top. They rolled up the windows and turned on the air conditioning. Asheris dropped into a low gear as the road dwindled to a bumpy, sandy track. Karissa surveyed the expanse of dun-colored sand dunes but saw nothing she recognized. Asheris continued the drive and after another hour, they passed through a vaguely familiar outcropping of sandstone.

"I think I remember that," she declared, nodding at the banded plateau. Her tongue, suddenly dry, stuck to the roof of her mouth.

"What do you remember about it?"

"The sphinx was near here. To the left, I think. Over there." She pointed to a sheltered cleft in the rock. Asheris steered the four-wheel drive to the cleft but found the passage barred by a boulder the size of a small sedan, as if someone had rolled it there to block the path. He turned off the engine and put his right hand on the door.

The sudden silence closed in on Karissa, allowing the haunting wail of the desert wind to whine around her soul, reminding her of the night so long ago when her world had fallen apart. She should never have come here with Asheris.

"Shall we get out and look?" he asked.

"I can't."

"You can, Karissa."

"I'd be an idiot to go near the sphinx again. What about the curse?"

Asheris sighed. "The only real curse was invoked by the High Priestess of Sekhmet and involved the commander-in-chief of the army. No one else."

"But what about my mother's death?"

"A coincidence, surely."

"And my father?"

"You tell me, Karissa."

"How can I, when I can't remember?" She passed the back of her hand across her damp forehead. "Maybe I don't even know what happened."

Asheris turned to her. "Is there anything you recall about the sphinx? Anything at all?"

"It was night. That's all I remember."

"That is all?"

Karissa glanced at him. "Didn't you mention that you were there that night, too? Don't you remember anything about the sphinx's location?"

"No. I was..." He glanced away as his voice trailed off in a vagueness that was at odds with his usual definite manner. "...I was not myself at the time."

"What do you mean? Were you ill or something?"

"I wasn't myself, that is all." He sent her a hard look that warned her not to press for more information. She glanced away, perplexed, and decided to ask him later what he meant.

He reached for her arm. "Please, Karissa, you must trust me when I tell you there is no curse. If you will only walk a while and look around, something might spark your memory. It is important that we find the lost sphinx as quickly as possible."

She pulled her arm away. "Can't you get it into your head that I don't want to remember?" Her voice rang sharp with anger.

He paused, as if he possessed infinite patience, even after her outburst, and stared into her eyes for a long moment. "To remember is to start to recapture yourself. To heal."

Frustrated, she glared at the dusty windshield with narrowed eyes. Would the man never give up?

"If you cannot do it for yourself, then do it for Senefret."

Her resolve to stay in the Land Rover faltered. Why did he have to remind her of the tragic priestess? Protecting her sanity was one thing. Refusing to help a stranded soul was the most selfish act she could imagine. She let out an exasperated breath.

"All right! But I can't guarantee anything." Karissa snatched her hat from the back seat, opened the door, and jumped out, prepared for the searing heat of the sand. Though Asheris was a persistent, irritating man, at least he had sent his manservant to purchase hiking boots and cotton clothing for her before they left Luxor, to make sure she had protection against the inhospitable desert. She plopped the hat on her head and looked up to find Asheris studying her.

He smiled at her as he slipped the keys in his pocket, obviously approving of the way she looked in her khakis. Trying not to think of his magnetic eyes or the way he had just manipulated her into helping him, she stomped toward the narrow cleft in the rocks. He walked beside her without making a sound.

Karissa plodded through the sand, squinting in the bright sun and trying to breathe in the oppressive heat. She hoped she would see something familiar in front of her so she wouldn't have to look back at events when the sphinx collapsed. But the longer she stared at the rock outcropping and the dunes beyond, the less certain she became that she had ever set foot in the area. At the edge of the outcropping, where strewn rock gave way to the endless desert sand, Karissa stopped and pushed back her hat.

"Are those backhoes over there?" she asked, pointing to the outlines of sand-blasted yellow machinery about a half-mile away.

"Yes. Mustofa has brought equipment out here to search. And should he find the entrance to the Valley of the Damned before we do, he will take everything without regard to ownership, and sell it on the black market to the highest bidder."

"Maybe Mustofa knows something we don't. And that's why he's digging over there."

"No. I am certain that Mustofa knows very little. He has just made a good guess as to the general area."

"Well, I don't recognize anything." She surveyed the dunes once more. "Sorry."

"Nothing?"

"Nothing." She turned and was surprised to find Asheris directly behind her. Was he trying to block her return to the Land Rover? Karissa glared at him. "Excuse me," she announced, taking a step as if to plow through him.

"Wait." He reached for her shoulders and enclosed them in a gentle but restraining hold. "Just for a moment."

"It's almost four o'clock. I could still catch my plane."

"You can get a flight in the morning."

"I want to leave now."

"After you have come so far? Come into the shade and talk to me for a moment. Over here." He urged her to walk toward a shady crevice in the rock. Karissa spied a metallic glint at the base. Could there be water? She would love to dip her hands in some water.

"All right," she followed him. "But just for a moment."

There was indeed a small pool at the base of the rock and a patch of grass. Karissa hunkered down, untied the scarf from her neck and dipped it in the water. She used the wet cotton to wipe her face and neck.

Asheris leaned against a nearby rock and watched her. "Tell me of your mother," he said.

She glanced up in surprise. "My mother?"

"Yes. Was she sick for a long time before her death?"

"No. She died from a strange fever that baffled the doctors. One day she was alive. The next, dead."

"Were your parents happy with each other?"

"My mother hated Egypt. She gave my dad a hard time about having to live here. They argued about that a lot."

"Did your father love your mother?"

"Yes...oh...I don't know." His questions made her nervous. She had asked herself the exact question a hundred times and wondered why she could never bring herself to examine her memory for an answer.

"Did your mother love him?"

"It was hard to tell. Grandmother Petrie often said that my mother rushed into marriage because of my father's good looks and charm. She warned me never to repeat the mistake."

"Marry in haste, may we repent at leisure, as they say?" Asheris lifted one brow.

"Perhaps." She suddenly wondered if she were in danger of repeating her mother's mistakes by falling precipitously in love with the attractive confident man who sat near the edge of the water.

Asheris picked up a pebble and tossed it into the pool. A series of rings blossomed outward and then drifted away to nothing. "Did you ever think that your father might have had a lot in common with his colleague, Dr. Raeburn?"

"Her?" Karissa pulled at the brim of her hat, mostly to hide her pinched expression. She didn't like discussing the strained relationship of her parents. "Gracie Raeburn was plain and dowdy. Why would my father be interested in her when he had someone like my mother? My mother was a beauty, you know."

"It may have been that your father valued Dr. Raeburn's mind and not her face. Your father may have enjoyed talking about his work with a woman who shared his love of archaeology."

"Why are you bringing this up?"

"So that you will consider what was going on between your parent and Dr. Raeburn when you were twelve years old."

"What are you implying?"

"Nothing. Perhaps if you think about your parents and Dr. Raeburn, you will begin to remember."

"There's nothing to remember."

Asheris took off his dark glasses and slipped them in the pocket of his shirt. He turned his intense gaze upon her, and she wondered if he intended to use his hypnotic eyes as a weapon.

"Karissa, you are fooling no one but yourself. There is a reason why you have let that night slip into blackness. I believe you saw something that greatly disturbed you."

"I saw nothing." She jumped to her feet as she pushed away a flashback, like a strobe light blinking on the sight of two people embracing, and then blinking off again. "I remember nothing! And don't try to put ideas in my head. It won't work."

She dusted off the knees of her khakis. The vision of the embrace in the sphinx flashed into her thoughts again, this time more slowly, giving her a glimpse of the expression on her father's face. She heard the echo of her young voice screaming in her thoughts. No-o-o-o! She saw her father glance in her direction, saw Gracie Raeburn twist in his arms. And then Karissa heard the ominous thud above their heads. Her heart twisted in her chest. She slammed her hat on her head and cut off the memory before it could rush to its horrifying climax.

Karissa dashed out of the tiny oasis, trying to outrun the memory. The possibility that she might relive the moments inside the sphinx made her desperate to escape. She couldn't endure witnessing it again, couldn't bear to think that she had been responsible for—

She broke off the thought and ran through the slipping sand. Her hat flew off, but she didn't care. All she could do was dash into the desert wilderness, hoping that if she went far enough and fast enough, she might outdistance the truth.

But she couldn't outdistance Asheris. He loped behind her, easily catching up with her, and grabbed at her arm to stop her. The movement knocked her off balance, and she fell, which sent her rolling down the slope of a dune. She slid to a stop at the bottom, but before she could scramble to her feet, she was pinned to the ground by Asheris. He forced her wrists to the sides of her head and straddled her legs with his knees.

She struggled to get away, but he held her firmly. After a few moments she surrendered and glared up at him. Only then did she realize her face was caked with tears and dust.

"Stop running, Karissa." His voice was much softer than the grip on her wrists. "It is time to see things for what they are."

"No!"

"Your father did not run off with Gracie Raeburn."

"Yes, he did. They were having an affair!"

"Who told you that?"

"My mother! She suspected it for years!"

"And you believed her?"

"Yes!" Karissa stared into his golden eyes. Damn those eyes. How could she escape the power of those eyes and the way they could pull her thoughts right out of her mouth. Her heart pounded in her chest, neck, and temples as the truth welled up inside her. She ran the tip of her tongue over her parched lips and saw Asheris watch the movement.

He bent down.

"No," Karissa began to whimper but his mouth closed over hers and cut off her protest.

"I am here now for you," he said against her lips. "Open your soul to me."

He kissed her in a lingering, thorough manner that set her heart racing all over again. Slowly he lowered himself until he sank down upon her, his firm chest to her breasts, his hard abdomen to her soft trim torso, and his lean legs stretched alongside hers. The weight of him made her body flare into full arousal, and the sheer size of him made her wonder if he might cover and consume her like a dark bird of prey. And his tongue! His tongue drove her mad. The surface of his tongue was quite raspy, which heightened the erotic sensation of every stroke. No man had ever done to her with his tongue what Asheris was doing now.

Karissa melted into the sand as Asheris moved over her in the first step of the sinuous dance between a man and a woman. She could feel the mark of his arousal, and when he surged against her and groaned, she felt her woman's blossom open, spreading its nectar deep inside her, preparing for the gift it ached to receive. She wanted to respond to him, wanted to wrap her arms around his muscular shoulders and pull him down to her lips. But he held her wrists above her head, and all she could do was gasp and moan as he bit her breasts through the cotton fabric of her shirt and bra, and arch upward as he kissed her throat and ears.

Open her soul to him? What did he mean? Did he want her to trust him enough to tell him everything she could remember so that he could drag even more memories to the surface? Or did he want her to open to him physically, and let him make love to her, here on the desert sand? How could she do either of those things? She had known Asheris for less than a week. How could she succumb to a man with such certainty?

Yet she knew she could trust him. And she knew she wanted him. There was no doubt in her mind that she wanted Asheris—in her arms, in her thoughts, and in the deepest place inside her. This need of him was elemental, undeniable, like breathing or eating. She had never felt so certain, not even with the man she had called her husband.

"Tell me now," he said, his voice husky.

"Tell you what?" She closed her eyes as he kissed her brow.

"Why you cannot face what happened that night."

An image as sharp as a knife blade sliced through her desire for Asheris. In the vision she saw her father look up, saw Gracie Raeburn slowly pull her arms from her father's shoulders.

"No!" she gasped.

"Tell me." He urged, rising to his knees. "What are you seeing?"

"Them together!"

"Who—your father and Dr. Raeburn?"

"Yes." She felt tears burning in her eyes. "I see them embracing. I see the look on my father's face."

"What kind of look?"

"It is—" She glanced at him and felt the corners of her mouth pulling down uncontrollably. She didn't want to break down, couldn't let herself break down. Not in all her therapy sessions had she come this close to cracking.

"It was what kind of look, Karissa?"

Karissa blinked through her tears and knew she was losing control. Something about Asheris' eyes induced her to spill her guts, to bare her soul, just as he had asked her to do.

She sighed and then whispered. "It is ecstasy."

Asheris' grip eased on her wrists. "Ecstasy because of Dr. Raeburn?"

"Why else?" Her voice was flat.

"There are joys other than sexual or romantic ones," he put in gently. "There is the joy of discovery."

"Joy of discovery?" She had never considered her father might have been embracing Gracie Raeburn for reasons other than sexual intimacy, especially after hearing her mother's views on the subject. Could she have been mistaken? Could she have seen ecstasy on her father's face and attributed it to love or lust, when all the time it had been out of the sheer joy of finding a grave site intact after years of searching? Ah, God—

"What else do you remember?" Asheris leaned closer. "Keep going!"

The vision came again, like a wave of nausea. She saw her father look up, saw Gracie Raeburn pull her arms from his shoulders as the sound of thunder filled the burial chamber.

The same thunder filled Karissa's mind, annihilating the hammering of her heart. She couldn't look any more, couldn't bear to hear the screams.

"No!"

"What do you see, Karissa? What is happening?"

"I screamed. I couldn't believe he would betray Mother like that. So, I started to yell. No-o-o!" She sank back, exhausted, as the words died on her lips.

"What did he do then?"

"Nothing. There was no time." She closed her eyes. Tears dropped down her temples and into her hair. "If I hadn't yelled, they might have had time. They might have been able to save themselves."

"From what?"

"From the block, the granite block that came down. Oh, God!" She turned her head and wept openly, unmindful of Asheris. Racking sobs rocked her torso. She longed to cover her face, but he kept her wrists trapped.

"Karissa." He kissed her left temple. "It was not your fault," he said. "You must know it was not your fault."

"It was! If I hadn't yelled, if I hadn't distracted them—"

"Many burial chambers are booby-trapped. Surely you know that."

"But if I hadn't yelled, they might have had time to get away!"

She shut her eyes, trying to blot out the image of the huge granite block, as big as a boxcar, which had come roaring out of the darkness. But this time there was no stopping the sight or the sound. This time she heard the horrified scream as the block of granite crushed her father and Dr. Raeburn, and then set into motion the disintegration of the sphinx, block by block, like dominoes. Karissa watched it all again and realized she was screaming and screaming and screaming.

Then someone lifted her to her feet and surrounded her in the warmth of a loving embrace. She let her head be held against a strong shoulder, let her waist be supported by the link of a powerful arm. She could neither stand nor speak or stop the flood of tears that poured from her eyes. Then that someone enfolded her to his human heart and murmured words no one had ever said to her—words she had desperately needed to hear when she was twelve years old and had just witnessed the gruesome death of her father.

That it was not her fault.

"Karissa, let it go. It was not your fault. You could not have known. It would have happened anyway. There was nothing you could have done to stop it. You are not to blame. Karissa, my sweet, let this darkness out of your heart. Let it go."

For sixteen years she had hidden the truth from everyone, including herself, that she had been responsible for the death of her father in the sphinx. For sixteen years she had lived with guilt so awful she couldn't face it. For sixteen years she had hung in an emotional limbo, frozen by the brand upon her child's heart that had damned her to a lifetime of unworthiness and self-recrimination. No one had been able to see the brand, but she had known it was there, every day, and the invisible scar had crippled her in so many ways.

But with each moment in the strong arms that held her, she felt the scar dissolving, the jagged edges smoothing and uncoiling, while pain and anguish drained out of her as she wept. No one had ever held her or comforted her like this. Her grandmother had never guessed she concealed a dark secret and had been too uninterested or afraid to examine the source of Karissa's rebellious tirades and black silences.

So, who held her now? Who cared enough about her to hold her like this? She glanced up through her tears, half-surprised to find herself not in her grandmother's house in Baltimore sixteen years ago, but in the arms of an Egyptian man on the edge of the Eastern Desert.

He gazed down at her, his topaz eyes full of compassion, his expression intent with concern. His words echoed in her mind like a long-forgotten song. He had called her his sweet. No one had ever murmured an endearment to her like that and truly meant it. And even if they had, she wouldn't have felt worthy enough to accept it. Now, however, she could. Asheris had helped her see that she was not to blame for the tragedy so long ago. Her heart swelled with an almost painful surge of gratitude.

"It has gone?" he asked gently. "The darkness?"

She gazed at him, stunned that Asheris could have walked into her life and started her on the road to healing in a single day. She tried to smile, but the expression only reached her eyes. Wordlessly, she wrapped her arms around his torso and clutched him with all her strength. He had given her what no one else had offered. He had shown her the way to look at the past and forgive herself. New tears came, tears of release and relief this time, and he held her until the sobs subsided.

"Karissa?" he asked at last, pulling away to take a look at her face. "Are you a little better now?"

She reached up and stroked his cheek with her right hand, cherishing the man who had just guided her through the gates of her trauma and beyond. "I think so."

He turned his head and kissed her palm.

"Who are you?" she asked in wonder, reaching up with her other hand. Her eyelids felt hard and scratchy from crying. "How did you ever find me?"

"It was you who found me," he replied. "But that story is for another time."

"Why not now?"

"The light is fading. I must get you back to Luxor before nightfall."

"But what about the sphinx?"

"We will have to look for it another day." He stepped away. "Come. We must hurry." He held out his hand to help her back up the slope.

Karissa reached for him and took a step, but dragged her feet because she was in no hurry to leave. Why was he suddenly so pressed for time? There was plenty of light to search for the lost sphinx. They might end up arriving in Luxor after dark, but why would that matter? His behavior was at odds with his insistence that they find the sphinx as soon as possible. She didn't quite know what to make of it. With her second step, her boot hit something hard in the sand, and she looked down. The corner of a piece of red granite stuck out of the dune.

"Wait!" she exclaimed. Karissa drew him back down the slope and then knelt on the sand. "Asheris, look!"

Chapter Six

Asheris dropped to his knees beside her and brushed away the sand to expose a block of pink granite. Nearby, Karissa toed through the sand, searching for another block and quickly finding one. She glanced up and met Asheris' gleaming eyes.

"Could this be it?" she gasped.

"It might be! I am going to establish the bearings of the location." He scrambled up the dune and pulled a compass out of his pants pocket. Keeping the rise of the rock formation directly behind him, he held out the compass and noted the direction of the exposed granite blocks. Karissa joined him at the top of the dune and reached down for her discarded hat. The wind was harsher at the top of the dune, and she hoped they would leave soon.

"I will bring men out here to dig tomorrow," he declared. "And we will see if the blocks are truly part of the sphinx."

"And if so, what then?"

"We will find the underground corridor that leads from the sphinx to the necropolis of the Valley of the Damned."

"The necropolis is underground?"

"Yes. The sphinx was built to guard it. Like any other sphinx."

Karissa smiled. Though she was emotionally drained, she was aware of Asheris' excitement. "That would be something, if we've really come across the lost sphinx just like that, by accident."

"Not by accident." He smiled down at her and dropped the compass in the pocket of his pants. "You brought us here."

"You had a hand in it, too," she countered. "If not for you, Asheris, I would still be running out in the desert. You helped me find the part of me that was lost, and in so doing, found these blocks."

"That part of you was there all along." He reached for her elbow and the gentleness in his voice turned to briskness. "Come. It grows late, Karissa. And I must be back before nightfall."

"Why?"

"I have business to attend to. And much to arrange."

"What do you do for a living, anyway?" she asked as they hurried toward the Land Rover. It was easier to talk of his life and interests than let her mind drift back to the night of the sphinx collapse.

"I am an antiquities dealer. I also lecture at the university here in Luxor and in Cairo, as well as in Europe." He pulled open the door of the vehicle and held it for her.

She got in and glanced at him. "As an expert in Egyptian artifacts?"

"Partly. I am considered an authority on the history of the Middle Kingdom." He closed her door and walked around to the other side of the Land Rover.

"My father would have enjoyed talking with you."

"As I would have enjoyed talking to him." He backed up the four-wheel drive and made a wide turn to head back to the main road. "I would have asked him what naughty things you did when you were a little girl."

"Me?" She smiled, feeling lighter now. "Naughty?"

"Yes, you." He cocked an eyebrow and looked over the top of his sunglasses at her. "You kiss like a naughty girl."

"Oh, really?" She tried to repress an outright grin.

"Like you know what you want from a man."

"That isn't being naughty, Mr. Asher, that's being honest."

"Oh? And what truths do your kisses tell?"

"I think you know, because you kiss like a wicked little boy."

"Ah." He smiled his slow smile when he realized she had thrown his taunting words back at him. The smile broadened as he turned his attention to the road. His teeth were very white in contrast to his skin.

Something warm and wonderful twisted inside her. Karissa gazed out the window, emotionally depleted but aware of a tantalizing prospect of happiness lurking at the edge of her exhaustion. Perhaps tonight, after she had rested and he had concluded his business, she could spend some time with Asheris before she left for Baltimore the next day. She could suggest celebrating the discovery of the lost sphinx and let the evening develop from there. She couldn't imagine leaving Luxor without telling him how much it meant to her when he had held her in his arms and given her comfort. She hoped she could spend her last hours in Egypt with him.

The only lover she had known had been her husband, and to define his perfunctory rituals in bed as lovemaking was to defile the very essence of the word. Thomas had been an indefatigable partner, determined to last as long as humanly possible before reaching a climax. But in his obsession with his own performance, he forgot the importance of touching, of exchanging whispered words of love, of conveying rich emotion through kisses of exquisite tenderness—the kind of kisses Asheris had already given her.

Instinctively, Karissa had known there could be much more between a man and woman than the mechanical coupling she had experienced with Thomas, but not until meeting Asheris had she desired to explore real lovemaking. Now she thought she would wither away with disappointment if she missed the chance to make love with the man beside her.

With Asheris, she would be making love, because her feelings for him grew deeper and broader with every kindness he showed her, every way in which he touched her, every time he kissed her. He seemed genuine. He seemed real.

She sighed and crossed her arms over her chest. She would be a fool if she let herself fall for a man who lived a world away from her home in Baltimore. She was crazy to think a man from another culture could be a good choice as a partner. But did she have a choice? Her heart knew no boundaries, geographically or culturally, and it was begging her to have faith in Asheris. She had spent a lifetime ignoring her inner voice. Perhaps it was time to listen.

Soon after they arrived back at Asheris' walled estate, he left to tend to his business affairs. Karissa called Josh to tell him of her change in travel plans, but once again was forced to leave a message on his answering machine. She wondered if the man was ever home. She hung up the phone, realizing she hadn't given a definite date for her return. Was she secretly hoping Asheris would ask her to stay for a few more days? She really couldn't stay, no matter how badly she wanted to get to know

Asheris. She had spent the last sixteen years totally devoted to her career. She couldn't throw it all away by being unprepared for the PBS special. However, something told her that because of Asheris, her life was about to expand beyond her career. Never again would she be satisfied with just her work.

Now that she thought about it, she felt even more driven to spend the last few hours with Asheris. To pass the time, Karissa took a long bath, luxuriating in the large sunken tub and savoring the foreign sensation of well-being that had begun to flicker in the center of her soul. She emerged from her bath, dressed in another of the delicate linen sheaths Eisha had laid out for her, and slipped on the armbands and necklace that had been placed there as well. The jewelry seemed to be very old, crafted of gold-colored metal and colorful gems, probably paste imitations of carnelians and emeralds, and real pieces of lapis lazuli. The wide colorful collar suited the dress and set off her complexion. Karissa glanced at herself in the mirror and was shocked to see how closely she resembled the female figures she had seen painted on the walls of tombs. Her Egyptian blood had never been as obvious as now when she was dressed in the garments of another age.

Karissa continued to stare. The garment felt right on her body. The jewelry draped perfectly across her shoulders and over her breasts. Even her black hair was cut in a blunt style across the middle of her back and above her eyebrows, just like the hair of the ladies she had seen in her father's books.

Sekhmet, Senefret, Asheris, Osiris. Why did the unusual names ring with such poignant familiarity? Was it because her father had been an Egyptologist and she had grown up on stories of the ancient world? Or did the familiarity spring from some fountain much deeper than her childhood? And why had Asheris provided her with these items of clothing? Was it for her pleasure or his? And if his, whose image did he see when he looked at her?

Perhaps, like her, Asheris was obsessed with a vision from the past. He didn't seem like the type of man to be possessed by a fantasy, but why else would he want her to dress in ancient clothing? She suspected the image from the past was Senefret. But why such an obsession for a person so long dead? Couldn't he be satisfied with a real life-and-blood woman?

Frowning, Karissa slipped off one armband, and was infused with a strange mélange of hurt and resentment for his disinterest in seeing her for herself. But she refused to let the hurt consume her. She would demand the truth from Asheris as soon as he came back for the evening.

Shaken and angry, she walked to the table near the door, picked up the brass bell, and rang it sharply. "Eisha!" she called.

Moments later, Eisha bustled through the open door.

"Yes, Miss Spencer?"

"Where are my clothes?" she asked.

"What clothes?"

"The *galabia* I was wearing when I came here the other night."

"That?" A confused expression passed through Eisha's dark brown eyes. "But that was just a rag."

"What did you do with it?"

"I threw it away, Miss Spencer." She glanced at the linen dress Karissa wore. "Do you not wish to wear the dress?"

"No. What about those khaki pants I had on this afternoon?"

"They are dirty. They must be laundered."

Karissa's frown deepened.

"Is there something wrong with the gown?" Eisha asked, tilting her head to inspect it.

"Yes. I feel as if I'm dressing in someone else's wardrobe. Who does this dress belong to?"

"I don't know." Eisha wrung her hands, obviously worried that Karissa was upset. "Mr. Asher selected it from his collection for you to wear."

"What collection?"

"His artifact collection."

"Is the collection in the house?"

Eisha looked over her shoulder as if worried that she might be overheard. "Yes."

"Would you take me to see it?"

"Mr. Asher likes to personally show the collection to guests."

"I don't think Mr. Asher will have enough time. And I would really like to see it before I leave tomorrow. Please."

Eisha glanced at her and then sighed. "All right, Miss Spencer. Follow me."

The housekeeper led her down a corridor, into a darkened wing of the house on the other side of the garden, and down a few steps. She selected a key from a ring on her belt and turned an ornate lock. Then she opened the door, flipped on the subdued lighting and held the door open for Karissa to pass through.

Karissa stepped into the room, awestruck. In pools of light, much like the arrangement of her gallery, she saw polished statues of granite, tables of ebony and ivory, boxes of all shapes, chairs with lion feet for legs, alabaster chalices, and ancient instruments that looked like simple harps. But what caught her attention the most was a glass case at the end of the room in which a life-size figure of a woman stood bathed in light. Karissa flowed closer with Eisha at her heels.

When she got close enough to make out the features of the woman, she stopped abruptly, shocked by the resemblance between the figure and her own appearance. The woman had long black hair, a slender face with wide dark eyes, delicate nose, and full lips. She was dressed in a sheath identical to the one Karissa was wearing.

"Who is this?" Karissa inquired, her voice hushed.

"A statue of an ancient one," Eisha replied. "The master had it carved by a French sculptor years ago."

"But who is she?"

"She was known as Senefret, a priestess of the Temple of Sekhmet."

Karissa stared up at the beautiful, haughty face of the priestess. Asheris was obsessed with the woman, and the only reason he was attracted to her was because of her similarity to Senefret. Her heart wrenched with dismay. Karissa glanced down at the dress she wore and then back up to the housekeeper. "I am dressed exactly like her."

"You look much like her," Eisha observed. "Strikingly so."

"Is this dress something she might have worn?"

"Yes. As I said, it came from this collection."

"So, I'm wearing a priceless artifact?"

"Yes."

Karissa held up her arm and stared at the golden band. "And what of this? Is the armband real, too?"

"Yes, Miss Spencer."

Karissa felt a chill pass over her, even though the evening was still balmy. "This jewelry is probably solid gold."

Eisha nodded.

"This is crazy." Karissa slipped the golden band down her arm and off her hand. "Do you have something practical to wear, Eisha? I don't care if it is one of Mr. Asher's shirts. Please, just get me something practical until the khakis are laundered."

"As you wish. This will not make Mr. Asher happy, however."

"Mr. Asher won't be happy if I ruin these, either."

She reached for the strings of the necklace where they were tied together at the nape of her neck. The sooner she got out of the ancient garments, the better. She wasn't certain why she was driven by the need to take off the clothing, whether because of Asheris' peculiar devotion to Senefret or the claustrophobic feeling the ancient dress and jewelry invoked in her. She looked up to find Eisha staring at her.

"I'm going back to my room," Karissa said. "Would you please find me something else to wear and bring it there?"

"Certainly. At once." Eisha ducked out of the room to do Karissa's bidding.

Karissa found her way back to her chamber and waited until Eisha appeared with a shirt and a light cotton robe, both masculine pieces. Then she left, allowing Karissa to dress, and returned a few minutes later with the evening meal and a babble of apologies.

"I thought you might like to eat in here," she explained, carrying the food to the table, "since you don't have proper attire for the dining room."

"Thanks." Karissa saw the single plate on the tray and wished she didn't have to eat alone, even though her sentiments regarding Asheris had taken a sudden turn. "Isn't Mr. Asher dining at home this evening?"

"No. Mr. Asher is never home in the evening."

"Oh." The comment deflated her even more. But she quickly replaced her disappointment with anger. Anger was a much less vulnerable way to deal with a man like Asheris. "Does he usually stay out late?"

"Quite late."

So much for her plans to ask him about the clothes. It was obvious he would not grace her with his company this evening. It was for the best anyway. Whenever Asheris was close at hand, she fell under his spell. It was better for both of them that they keep their distance.

Karissa sat down at the table. The clothing Eisha had brought her smelled faintly of Asheris. She tried to ignore the light musky fragrance, but his scent made her pause for a moment and think of his kiss and his arms. Then Eisha put an aromatic plate of rice, lamb, and vegetables in front of her, and the smell of the food brought her back to her senses. A folded newspaper lay on the tray.

"Would you like to read the paper?" Eisha asked, holding it out. "It is an English version."

"Yes. Thank you."

"I thought you might like to read while you eat, as Mr. Asher has no television in the house."

"Thank you, Eisha." Karissa took the paper. "That is kind of you."

A minor headline at the bottom of the page caught her eye. Man mauled by cat. She scanned the article and realized she was reading an account of the panther attack on the man who had tried to rape her. The succulent lamb caught in her throat as she continued to read. The article mentioned the name Lord Azhur, partially attributing the death to him. Who was this mysterious lord and what did he have to do with the panther?

Karissa glanced up from the paper to find Eisha folding the linen dress near the bed.

"Eisha," Karissa began. "Tell me, do you know anything about a person named Lord Azhur?"

"Lord Azhur?" Eisha's hands paused for a moment, but she didn't look up from her task.

"Yes. I've heard that name twice now, and here it is in the paper. Who is Lord Azhur?"

Eisha picked up the golden armband. "He is a character in our folklore."

"In your folklore? But why would someone being attacked by the man-killing panther call out the name of Lord Azhur?"

"Because Lord Azhur is said to be half-man and half-panther. And that is whom they believe is attacking them."

"That sounds far-fetched."

"Not to an Egyptian. Many of our ancient gods had the bodies of men and the heads of birds or animals. Perhaps they were half-man and half-beast as well."

"But we're not speaking of ancient gods, here, Eisha. We're talking about a panther attack in modern day."

"I know." Eisha nodded. "It has been rumored that Lord Azhur walks the earth again as he did thousands of years ago.

There have been reports such as that one in the paper for many years now."

"And no one has caught the cat?"

"No." Eisha took the dress and jewelry to the door. "But no one has tried very hard to capture him, Miss Spencer, for it seems those who are killed by Lord Azhur are unsavory characters, criminals—all evil men."

Karissa chewed thoughtfully.

Eisha continued. "Lord Azhur does what our police sometimes fail to achieve."

"But isn't anyone curious to find out who or what this Lord Azhur really is?"

"He is a spirit, Miss Spencer, doomed to walk the earth for eternity. The Arabs named him when they first came across him in the desert. They soon learned to fear him. In fact, there are places that no man will go after sunset in the Eastern Desert."

"Why?"

"Because Lord Azhur haunts the desert there. Some say he guards ancient tombs, and that he will kill all who venture close to the valley where the tombs are said to be."

"But he is the one who brought me here. It must have been him. A panther saved my life and led me to this house."

"A panther?"

"Yes. I followed him for miles. He was in the United States too, I'm sure of it. And he never once threatened me."

"I do not know how to explain it."

Karissa stirred her rice with her fork. She recalled the story Asheris had told her of the commander who had been cursed by the High Priestess of Sekhmet, mummified alive, and then partially redeemed by Osiris. If the panther was more than just a simple creature, he might be the same cat Asheris had mentioned in his tale. And if the cat was the wandering spirit of the man buried alive, of course he would have wanted to protect the single human being who knew about the lost sphinx. And he would have brought her to the house of the modern man who was intent on finding the sphinx as well. It all made sense. The only part that wasn't easily explained was Asheris' connection to the sphinx and his uncommon loyalty to a woman long dead.

Karissa decided not to brood upon the subject. She would ask Asheris about it in the morning.

The next day she rose and padded across the tiled floor to the balcony. Just as before, she looked down to find a dead bird, this time a hoopoe bird. Karissa glanced around the sunny garden, even though she was certain she would see no sign of the cat that had left her the gift. She assumed the panther had brought the bird to her, just like the other times. Cats often gave their owners presents such as this as a symbol of love and respect. Did the panther have such feelings for her? She hoped not. She wasn't too crazy about the possibility that a man-eating cat considered her part of his "family." Karissa turned away and went back into the bedchamber.

Eisha came in a few minutes later with her clean khaki pants and cotton shirt and a promise to send someone out to buy her more suitable apparel later that morning.

Karissa took her breakfast in the garden, surrounded by the caged birds, who were all singing and chattering. The air was completely still and pleasantly warm and held a shimmering promise of the blessed day to come. Karissa tipped her face to the sky and savored the moment. The mornings and evenings were her favorite times of the day in Egypt, both far different from any she had enjoyed in the States. She felt a wave of homesickness, not for Baltimore, but for her days in Luxor, when she had been a child. How she had loved it here! And how she would hate to leave.

Long after ten o'clock, Eisha came back to clear away the breakfast dishes. She chatted brightly about the garden as she put the plates on a tray, and Karissa listened, half amused. She wondered if Eisha had been longing for female company, for she was never in a hurry to break off their conversations. Karissa didn't mind, though, because she had to wait for two hours until Asheris emerged from his chamber, and those two hours seemed days away.

Soon, however, Eisha cocked her head. "The doorbell," she declared. "Mr. Asher must have a visitor. Excuse me."

Karissa nodded and looked at her watch as Eisha hurried out of the room. Ten-fifteen. Who could be visiting Mr. Asher at this early hour?

She finished her coffee just as Eisha returned.

"Miss Spencer?" she said, "There's a gentleman to see you."

Chapter Seven

"A man?" Karissa questioned, rising to her feet. Would Mustofa have the audacity to come here? "Did he give his name?"

"He said his name was Mr. Lambert."

Josh? Karissa couldn't believe Josh had come all the way from Baltimore after having received her first message. He must have been traveling nonstop ever since, and he must have paid a premium for tickets, too. She was relieved that her visitor was Josh and not Mustofa, but she wasn't too pleased that Josh had dropped everything to fly to Egypt when it wasn't necessary.

"Shall I show him in?" Eisha added.

"Yes. And bring some coffee, please?" Karissa motioned toward the empty carafe. "I'm sure Mr. Lambert will be in need of refreshment."

"Certainly." Eisha hurried off and returned with a slightly disheveled, stubble-cheeked Josh.

As soon as he caught sight of Karissa, he strode forward, swiping palm fronds out of his way and tripping on the uneven tile of the old garden.

"Josh," she greeted. "What are you doing here?"

"I was worried." He grabbed both her hands and held her out in front of him. "Are you okay?"

"Yes." In fact, she was better than she had been in a long while, but she decided not to mention it. She slipped her hands out of his grasp. "I'm fine."

"So, what happened? Did that Mr. Asher snatch you out of the gallery?"

"No. I told you on the answering machine that a man named Mustofa kidnapped me. Mr. Asher has been very accommodating."

"But why? Why were you kidnapped?"

Karissa briefly explained about the lost sphinx and the buried tombs, omitting any reference to Asheris' story about Senefret.

"So how did you get away from Mustofa?"

"Believe it or not, a black panther rescued me."

"A black panther? You mean like the one we saw in Baltimore?"

Karissa nodded. Eisha swept forward with a tray of coffee, dates, and sweet breads. Karissa introduced Josh to the housekeeper and then motioned for him to sit down.

"The locals believe the cat is part of Egyptian folklore, a half-man half-panther named Lord Azhur."

"So, what was he doing in Baltimore? Vacationing?" Josh popped a date in his mouth.

Karissa glanced at him, wanting more than anything to bounce what she was feeling and what she had learned about Asheris off someone who knew her, someone she could trust. But though Josh was a longtime friend, he just wasn't the type of person she could confide in. He could be endearing, but he was often more like a basset hound tripping on his own droopy ears than a man of thirty-two. So, she sighed and decided to keep her own counsel. Besides, she should trust her own judgment, not someone else's.

"Everyone thinks I can remember the location of the lost sphinx," she explained, "including Lord Azhur. That's why he protected me, I assume."

"Hmmm." Josh took a long swig of coffee. "So, what are you planning to do?"

"I was planning to fly back to Baltimore, either today or tomorrow."

"Oh."

"There really wasn't any need for you to come all this way, Josh."

"I was worried about you." He reached across the table and put his hand over hers. She let her hand remain, but all the while wanted to pull away. "I couldn't sleep thinking my favorite sculptress might be in danger."

"I appreciate it, Josh, but I'm fine. And you shouldn't have gone to so much expense on my account."

"There are times when money is no object."

He gazed at her, with a crazy smile on his lips that made him look like a lovesick puppy. Karissa slipped her hand away, wanting to ask him if money was ever the object with him, but not wishing to hurt his feelings. That would be too nasty after all the hours he had spent traveling to her side.

She was about to suggest that Josh freshen up and take a nap when she saw his smile freeze and his gaze travel upward to somewhere above her head.

Karissa turned, just as two elegant hands slipped around the corners of the back of her chair. Asheris had come up behind her, and yet she hadn't heard the slightest sound of his approach. She glanced up at him, struck by his dark, handsome face and bemused by the way he stood behind her, as if laying claim to the space between him and Josh, which included her and the chair.

"I thought I heard a stranger's voice in my garden," Asheris said.

"This is my business partner, Josh Lambert," Karissa remarked, turning back to the table. "Josh, this is Mr. Asher, whom you may remember from the gallery?"

"Right." Josh pushed to his feet, forgetting his napkin, which fell to the ground. Flustered, he reached down, picked it up, and then offered his hand to Asheris, realizing too late that he still held the linen. Blushing and grinning, he transferred it to his other hand.

"How do you do?" Josh asked.

Asheris didn't move from his stance behind Karissa, which forced Josh to step forward and lean into the handshake. The subtle power play was not lost on Karissa. She sat back, allowing her weight to sink against Asheris' left hand. His long slender fingers pressed into her shoulder.

"Mr. Lambert." Asheris paused as if judging Josh in some way. "What brings you to my country?"

"Karissa does, actually."

"Oh?" Asheris returned his right hand to the back of her chair.

"I was worried about her. I wanted to make sure she was all right."

"It is my hope that Karissa considers herself well taken care of."

"I do," she put in. A warm flood passed over Karissa. She was being taken care of, better than anyone had cared for her in her entire life. Though she had never lacked in the physical needs department in the home of Grandmother Petrie, she had never been given understanding and compassion, both of which Asheris offered in abundance.

"Even so." Josh put his napkin on the table. "I still want to accompany you back home, Karissa, to make sure that Mustofa character doesn't threaten you again."

"Until she leaves, you are welcome to stay here as my guest, Mr. Lambert."

"Really? That would be great."

"In fact, you must be tired after your long journey. Would you care to rest for a few hours and refresh yourself?"

"As a matter of fact, I would. I'm dog tired!"

Asheris slipped his hands free and clapped them. Eisha appeared a few moments later. "Would you show Mr. Lambert to a guest room, Eisha," he said. "He will be staying with us temporarily."

"Very good, Mr. Asher." Eisha turned to Josh. "Would you follow me, sir?"

"Catch you later, Karissa," Josh said, taking another date from the tray. "And thanks, Asher."

Asheris nodded slightly.

Josh strode after Eisha while Asheris lowered his hands, but this time his palms came to rest on the tops of Karissa's shoulders. She thrilled to his touch. Before she could say anything, however, he lowered his head and pressed a tender kiss near her ear. Goose bumps burst on her arms and across her back.

"You are unquestionably," he said, "the loveliest creature in my garden."

She flushed with pleasure at his words. "Thank you," she murmured.

"It was nice to awaken to the sound of your voice." He brushed back her hair and kissed her neck, and she couldn't resist inclining her head to allow him room for more kisses. His lips ventured across her neck as his hands slid down the front of her cotton shirt to caress her breasts. A sigh escaped her, and she tipped her head back against his shoulder as he hovered over her.

"Asheris," she gasped, almost forgetting her intention to question him about his control of her wardrobe. "You're up early, aren't you?"

"Yes. I am up," he murmured in her ear. "Very much so."

She flushed again, wishing the back of the chair was not there to separate them.

"Was I talking too loudly?" she asked, trying not to succumb to his mouth, but having little success. She thought she would melt into the chair. "Did I wake you?"

"Exquisitely." He eased a warm hand into the opening of her shirt, slipped his fingers into her lacy bra, and flicked her nipple, which sent a delightful spiral of sensation right down to her womanhood. "And do I not awaken you as well?"

"Yes." She couldn't bear the one-sided embrace for another instant. Twisting around, she stood up and rose into his arms, and he took her in a fluid motion.

Hungrily their mouths came together as her arms went around his neck. He slid his hands down her back and pulled her hips to his. In a moment she was fused into him, her breath coming fast and hard as he crushed her against his straining body. Their kisses turned into a frenzy of tongues and lips, of passionate nips and ragged sighs. Karissa wanted him so fiercely that she didn't care if they sank to the tile and made love then and there, in broad daylight. She longed to consume him and be consumed in return, and the sharp need for him made her moan out loud.

"Karissa," he gasped. "I ache for you."

She half-opened her eyes, nearly overcome by the need to join her body and soul to his. But she could not forget the clothes and the doubt that nagged her, making her wonder about Asheris' motives. She couldn't give herself freely as long as doubt held her back.

"Is it me you ache for," she murmured, "Or another?"

He pulled away from her mouth, and she felt his body tense.

She glanced up, anxious to read his expression before he could hide his initial reaction. Asheris' face was full of surprise and then wariness. His wariness was all she needed to answer her question and cool the flames of her desire.

"I do remind you of someone," she said, her voice breaking. "It isn't me you want, is it?"

"Yes, it is." He tried to pull her closer, but she pushed against his chest.

"Let me go," she demanded miserably. "Please, Asheris."

"Karissa, do not pull away from me!"

"I have to!" she stepped back, and he reluctantly loosened his hold on her. "I knew by those dresses you gave me to wear that I reminded you of someone else. But I'm not playing second fiddle to anyone again. Not ever!"

"You are not playing second fiddle, Karissa. I do not know how to explain it, but there is something about you—"

"That reminds you of that priestess, right?" Karissa wrenched out of his grip. "That's why you came on to me so strong, so quickly."

"It is much more than that. You must believe me."

"Why should I? You're just like Thomas, looking at me and wishing you were with someone else. Maybe all men are like that. Who knows! And who gives a good God-damn!" She broke into a sob and whirled away, stumbling blindly through the garden. Men could go to hell. Thomas, Josh, and Asheris—all of them.

He loped up behind her. "Karissa, please, you must listen to reason."

"Go to hell!" she cried. "I'm leaving!"

"Do not do this. You must not leave me like this."

"Why not?" She turned at the door. "I have better things to do with my life than serve as a stand-in for other women. How do you think that makes me feel?"

He paused, struggling for something to say to convince her to stay. The look on his face was so desperate that for a moment she almost believed he truly cared about her. Then logic and pride brought her back to her senses.

"I thank you for your hospitality," she said. "But I'm taking the first flight out of Luxor. If the blocks turn out to be the lost sphinx, you can mail me a check. I assume you have my address in your files."

Asheris sighed. "There are reasons for my conduct," he declared. "I am not able to tell you everything about my life. I only ask that you have faith in my actions and trust in what you feel for me."

"I've been fooled before, Mr. Asher, and it isn't worth the disappointment."

"I am not trying to fool you, Karissa. What I feel for you is unbelievably real, unbelievably good. Surely you can see that."

"No. Sorry."

"Then you are lying to yourself again."

"Who has been lying to whom?" She glared at him, her emotions roiling, unable to trust her feelings or the motives of a handsome man.

"You cannot go." Asher reached for her arm just as Josh appeared in the doorway.

"Keep your hands off her!" Josh demanded, lunging for the Egyptian. He would have knocked Asheris to the ground but for the Egyptian's finely honed reflexes. Asheris quickly stepped to the side and out of Josh's path. Josh stumbled through thin air but didn't lose his balance. He spun around, angry and breathing hard.

"I knew there was something funny going on around here!"

"Josh!" Karissa exclaimed. She didn't want him involved in her personal affairs with Asheris and hated to see the Egyptian have the chance to make a fool out of him. She dashed to Josh's side and took his arm. "It's okay."

"No, it isn't okay! This asshole thinks he can push you around. And I don't like it."

"I have not made Karissa do anything against her will," Asheris put in calmly.

"I'll bet. I saw the way you just grabbed her and heard what you said. She doesn't have to stay here another minute. She can damn well leave whenever she pleases!"

"Yes." Karissa raised her chin. The best solution was to leave Asheris' house and go to a hotel downtown. From there she could make travel arrangements, leave Asheris and Egypt far behind, and get back to her regular life. "Get your bags, Josh. I'll call a cab." She turned to Asheris, "If I may be permitted the use of your phone."

"Of course." His eyes glittered at her. "You know I can refuse you nothing."

For a moment their eyes locked and held, and Karissa had her first glimpse of Asheris' wrath. The warmth she was accustomed to seeing in his eyes had vanished. In its place was a cloud of stormy topaz, so cold and unemotional that she shuddered at the force of it.

Without another word, Asheris brushed past her and strode into the house.

As impossible as it seemed, Karissa couldn't get a flight out of Luxor that day and was forced to make reservations for the next afternoon. She and Josh got rooms at the Blue Palace Hotel and spent the rest of the day cruising the bazaars. When the merchants took their afternoon break, Karissa retired to her room to work on her interview presentation. She didn't emerge until dinner, which she and Josh had agreed to share at the hotel restaurant at eight o'clock.

Josh was late, leaving Karissa to while away the minutes drinking a glass of wine and gazing across the glistening expanse of the Nile. She sat in the outdoor section, which was built of white stone overlooking the river. A balmy breeze drifted through her hair and ruffled the gauzy skirt she had purchased at a market stall. The evening air was a perfect temperature, the view was gorgeous, and the spicy smells of lamb and chicken wafting from the kitchen were heavenly. Even though she brooded over Asheris, she still enjoyed the ambiance of the hotel.

"Sorry I'm late!" Josh declared as he strode up to the table, startling her out of her thoughts. "I had an important errand to run." He wiggled his eyebrows and opened his suit jacket, just enough to permit her a quick view of a handgun stuck in his waistband.

Karissa watched in concern as he rebuttoned the jacket. "Why did you get that?"

"I have a feeling we aren't through with your Egyptian friend yet. And the next time I confront him, I'm going to have a little firepower to back me up." Josh plopped down in his chair. "You wouldn't believe how easy it was to get the sucker. And how cheap it was."

"I don't like guns, Josh."

"Well, neither do I. But I'll feel a whole lot safer with it." He picked up the menu. "Have you ordered?"

"No. I was waiting for you."

They ate dinner and chatted about the upcoming PBS special. Karissa couldn't help thinking about the lunch she had shared with Asheris, and how he had captivated her with his story. All Josh could do was crack jokes about flight attendants and complain about the airline food, claiming he had been served a roll that was as hard as a dog biscuit. When Josh got up to pay for dinner, Karissa wandered over to the edge of the balcony and leaned upon the warm stone, remembering the way Asheris had touched her and kissed her. She had almost been fooled into thinking he actually cared for her.

Josh wanted to check out the nightlife in Luxor, but Karissa declined, worried that she might be seen by Mustofa or Asheris. She wanted to turn in early anyway, because of the big travel day ahead of them. She walked back to her room and got ready for bed. She slipped on the khaki shirt, making it do double duty as a nightshirt. Then she made sure the door connecting her room with Josh's was locked, tucked her room key into the pocket of the shirt, and slipped between the cool sheets.

The bed smelled of heavy cologne, pine-scented air freshener, and cigarette smoke, a far cry from the freshly laundered scent of the bed linen at Asheris' home. The two days she had spent in the luxurious environment of his home had spoiled her. She sighed and lay back, wanting to forget the man, but knowing it would take a long time before her mind would be clear of him.

Karissa drifted off to sleep and didn't awaken until close to dawn, when a strange clicking sound brought her back to consciousness. She rose to her elbows, listening for the unfamiliar noise, and then saw the dark shape of a man outlined against the open doors of her balcony. Someone had come into her room by way of the French doors.

"Josh!" Karissa yelled.

At the sound of her voice, the dark shape bolted toward her. She scrambled out of the bed, tripping on the sheets, but caught herself to keep from falling to her hands and knees.

"Josh!" she screamed.

The man grabbed for her and missed. She glanced at his dark face beneath a mop of black hair and a huge moustache but didn't recognize him. Was he a thief or another of

Mustofa's thugs? Whoever he was, now that she had seen him, she was probably in serious trouble. For a moment she hesitated, unsure of where to go or what to do. The intruder's stocky body blocked her way to the main corridor, so she dashed to the balcony, praying that Josh had heard her.

Dressed only in the khaki shirt and her panties, she grabbed a hotel robe from the bed and raced through the French doors. She flung a leg over the side of the baluster and looked down at the one-story drop below. She would have to jump over the side and into a garden area that bordered the outdoor pool. With luck, however, she might run into someone to help her down below. Without much thought to personal injury, Karissa sat on the rail of the baluster and pushed off, just as the intruder burst onto the balcony. She landed with a hard thump in the sandy earth below and felt as if her knees had just jammed into her thighs.

She yanked on the robe and limped off, headed for the shadows along the side of the hotel. Behind her she heard the thud and gasp as the man with the moustache hit the ground behind her. She had only seconds to dash around to the front of the hotel, find the lobby, and ask for help.

Just then Josh hollered from above. The man with the moustache stopped and looked up, which gave Karissa time to race down the gravel path toward the front of the hotel. Then in the dawning light, she saw the locked gate in the wall. It made sense, since the path led to the pool, that the gate would be closed and locked to prevent drunken guests from accessing the water. Karissa's heart sank. The wall was too high for her to scale. And now the intruder had turned and was running toward her. She backed against the wall, trapped in a wrought iron box canyon.

Her heart leapt in her throat as the man ran up, a cruel smile on his face.

"Nowhere to run, American?" he asked.

She refused to answer him and wished she was wearing more clothing. If this man were anything like the last thug, he might attempt to assault her.

Karissa crossed the robe over her body, just as a black shape sailed through the air.

The black panther had come to her rescue again.

The cat hit the intruder in the center of his chest, knocking him backward to the ground. The man yelled and struggled with the big cat. He even managed to lumber to his feet and stumble into the bushes, but the panther leapt after him.

Josh careened around the corner, brandishing his handgun. "What's going on?" he cried.

"Lord Azhur went after the intruder!" Karissa pointed in the direction of the tangled undergrowth. Josh peered into the bushes, which were still quite shadowed even though light climbed in the eastern sky. In a few minutes the sun would show above the cliffs of the Eastern Desert.

"Stop!" Josh yelled. Still the man crashed through the shrubbery, blubbering in terror at being chased by an immense cat. A blood curdling snarl rent the air and the man broke free of the plants, a mere few feet from Josh.

Josh panicked and squeezed off a shot.

The bullet buried itself in the man's leg and sent him toppling to the ground. Over the body of the fallen man soared the panther, paws outstretched, headed for Josh. Aghast, he staggered backward and took another shot, hitting the cat before he fell onto the sand.

"No!" Karissa screamed.

The panther plunged to the ground and collapsed in the sand, panting heavily and trying in vain to regain his footing. Karissa watched him struggle and was filled with dismay when the beautiful animal could not rise. What damage had the bullet inflicted? She could see a red wound on the cat's left shoulder.

"Josh!" Karissa cried, appalled that he had hurt the panther. She ran toward the cat.

"Watch out," Josh warned. "It might be dangerous!"

"You shouldn't have shot it!" she exclaimed, sinking to her knees beside the animal. "How could you!"

"I thought it was going to get me!"

By that time, two men from the hotel came running around from the back. Karissa recognized the bellboy who had been on duty that evening and another man she had never seen, probably the night manager.

"What is going on?" the manager asked. "We heard gunshots."

"I caught this guy breaking into my partner's room," Josh explained, training his gun on the man with the moustache. "He needs to be turned over to the police."

"I will call them," the bellboy said, turning on his heel to return to the hotel.

"Bring him inside," the manager pointed at the bleeding man. Then he caught a glimpse of the dark shape in the shrubbery behind Karissa. "Is there someone else over there?" He stepped closer.

"No." Karissa shielded the panther from view. "Just my garment bag," she lied. "The thief tried to steal my things."

The manager stroked each side of his mustache with the curl of his right index finger, as if deciding whether the disturbance could be covered up easily, thereby restoring the decorum of his hotel. "Very well." Then he reached down and yanked the intruder to his feet. "Come along, you," he demanded. "You have much to explain."

Josh kept his gun trained on the intruder and walked him toward the back of the hotel, leaving Karissa to deal with the cat.

Desperate to help the creature, she glanced after Josh and the others as they disappeared around the corner of the building. She felt the first rays of sunlight on the back of her shirt and the calves of her bare legs. What could she do about the panther? Call a vet? And what would the veterinarian do once he discovered his patient was none other than the mankiller, Lord Azhur. Would the vet demand that the panther be put to sleep? She couldn't take the chance. And yet who else could help dig a slug out of a panther's shoulder?

Struggling with the dilemma of what she should do, Karissa pushed back the branches of a shrub, the sun like a spotlight now, so she could take a good look at the cat. But the panther had vanished. In its place was a tall slender man lying face down, his black hair tumbling over the crook of his arm, long lean legs splayed in the sand, and his shoulder bleeding profusely.

Then he moaned and turned to face her. For a moment Karissa couldn't speak, so great was her shock at seeing the man's familiar features.

Chapter Eight

"Asheris!" she exclaimed.

His eyelids fluttered. Then his eyes opened and found hers. "Karissa."

"It can't be! You—" She broke off, too shocked to complete the improbable thought. "You and the panther are—"

"A tale for later," he gasped. "Please, help me."

She jerked back to reality, back to the sight of the blood on his arm as well as in the sand. The ashen tint to his skin alarmed her. Now was not the time to ask him about the panther and what she thought had transpired a few moments ago. There was a real flesh and blood man on the ground in front of her who needed medical attention.

"Can you get up?" she asked.

"With your assistance."

She got to her feet and reached for his uninjured arm, leaning backward to pull him up. Slowly and shakily Asheris rose. As she watched him step out from under the shrub, she realized with another shock that he was completely naked. Though Karissa was worried about his condition, she couldn't help but notice the sculpted beauty of his torso and hips, and the dark hair that feathered from his belly and spread out at his loins. He was uncircumcised. She had never seen a natural man before.

She flushed at the sight of him and stripped off the white hotel robe she was wearing. She was dressed only in her shirt and panties, but the long shirttails were sufficient covering for the time being.

"Here," she said. "Let me put this on you." She eased the robe over him, taking care not to hurt his injured shoulder. He put his right arm through the sleeve, and she tied the belt around him.

"Thank you," he said.

"Come up to my room and I'll call a doctor."

He reached for her forearm. "No doctor."

"The police then."

"No police. Just you."

"But you've been shot!"

"I will be all right." He closed his eyes for an instant, as if fighting off a wave of pain or dizziness.

"Come on then." She slipped her arm around his waist. "The back door must be open by now."

He draped his right arm over her shoulders and leaned heavily upon her, as if most of his strength had drained away with his blood. She staggered for a moment until she found a rhythm in the way they walked together, and then guided him toward the back of the hotel. She prayed they wouldn't run into Josh, because she didn't want to have to explain Asheris' presence or the possibility that the Egyptian had transformed from a panther into a man.

They slipped in the back of the hotel and headed for the elevators. From across the lobby Karissa glimpsed Josh and an officer of the law walk into a room accompanied by the manager. Relieved that Josh was occupied, at least for a while, she pushed the button for the elevator. Perhaps she could get Asheris out of the hotel before Josh found out he had been there at all. She felt compelled to protect Asheris' secrets from everyone, even Josh.

Asheris was silent all the way to the room. Luckily Karissa had put her room key in the shirt pocket the night before. She unbuttoned the flap on her pocket and pulled out the key while Asheris stood beside her, pale and quiet.

"You need a stiff drink," she remarked, pushing the door open.

"Yes."

She shut the door and led him to the bed. He sank down on the mattress.

"Lie down and I'll have a look at your shoulder," she said.

Asheris lay back, his raven hair stark against the white pillow. Karissa loosened the robe and gently drew back the left side to reveal his shoulder.

She grimaced. "I'll have to clean it before I can see anything. But I'll get you that drink first." She rose and hurried to the bar near the television where small bottles of liquor were lined up by inverted glasses. She unscrewed the lid of a bottle of Jack Daniels and poured it into the glass. Then she returned to the bed.

"Here, Asheris." She handed the drink to him. Asheris took the glass in his right hand and rose up just enough to sip the bourbon.

"Thank you," he murmured.

"I'll get some soap and water," she said, heading for the bathroom. She was glad to have something important to do, because the sight of Asheris wounded disturbed her more than she would have guessed.

When she returned to the bedside, she could see the liquor had already affected him. His cheeks had more color in them, and his eyes were open and clear. She flipped on the lamp and sat down beside him, acutely conscious of the nearness of his body and the slightly spicy scent of his skin, as if he had dusted himself with coriander.

Carefully, she dabbed his shoulder with a wet washcloth until the ragged edges of the wound were visible. Asheris had been shot at such close range that there were powder burns on his skin.

"You're lucky," Karissa observed. "It looks as if the bullet just grazed you."

"Good. Just wrap my shoulder."

Karissa made a patch with a clean folded washcloth and tied it in place with strips of a torn pillowcase.

"Good," Asheris commented when she finished.

"Now what?" she asked. "Do you want to go home?"

"Yes. And I want you to come with me."

"I told you, Asheris, I have to go back to Baltimore."

"I must show you what was found yesterday." He looked into her eyes, and she felt the familiar hypnotic sensation melting away her resolve. She broke away from his gaze and stood up, determined to resist him, but his rich voice followed her. "Karissa, please come back with me."

"I'm not going anywhere with you until you explain some things first."

"Such as?"

"Such as who you really are."

Asheris sighed and lay against the pillows. The robe fell open above the belt to reveal the taut suppleness of his abdomen. Karissa glanced away from his torso and looked into his eyes instead.

"So?"

"So," he repeated tiredly. "Surely you must have guessed who I am."

"I think I have, but it's too outrageous to consider."

"Why?"

"Eisha told me about a legendary man who could change back and forth into an animal. But it's just a folk tale. It isn't possible."

"How do you know?"

"I've never seen it happen. No one has."

"No one has seen your god, yet many believe in him."

Karissa stared at Asheris, unable to refute his reasoning. He reached out and gently drew her back down beside him. She acquiesced and sat near his hip with her hand still in his.

"Karissa, there are powers possessed by some people that would astound you, especially in the days long ago when the mind of man was more open to possibilities than it is now. In my day, man was obsessed with the unknown and the fantastic, just as in this day, man is obsessed with facts and data." He paused and closed his eyes for a moment, as if gathering his strength, and then continued. "Unfortunately, while looking for proof and applying human rules to the universe, man has become rigid in his thinking, and has lost more knowledge than he has gained over the centuries, believe me."

"You're saying that we are more backward now than we used to be?"

"In some respects, very much so."

"And you're saying that a few thousand years ago, people knew how to change other people into animals?"

"Yes. Modern man holds himself apart from the animals, but in truth we are not that far from the beasts, you know."

"Then you are Lord Azhur."

He nodded.

"What were you doing here at the hotel?"

"I assume I was here as the panther, following Mustofa's man."

"Well, if you are Lord Azhur, you are also the man in the story you told me about, the one with the commander of the Egyptian army and the priestess Senefret."

"Yes. But you must tell no one."

She couldn't believe it. She was sitting on a bed talking with a man who had been mummified alive four thousand years ago, a man who had been searching for the woman he loved for centuries. Preposterous! Unbelievable. When she tried to pull her hand away, however, he clasped it firmly and drew it to his chest.

"I know you find my tale hard to believe, Karissa. But you must realize that I am telling you the truth."

"Why should I believe you?" she retorted. "How can you appear as a real man to me if you had been mummified alive?"

"I have been partially freed of my curse," he replied gently.

"How?"

"By you. When you came to the sphinx and shouted 'no,' you released me from my tomb, but not from the curse of being a panther."

"How could I do that?"

"I am not certain. I think it had something to do with the particular resonance of your voice and the single word you spoke."

"You mean I set up some sort of vibration in the sphinx?"

"Perhaps. I also believe you are somehow connected to my past, though in what capacity I am not sure."

"But if you are the panther, why couldn't you find the sphinx yourself? You saw where it was after it collapsed."

"I have no memory of the time I spend as a panther."

"You don't know what you do when you're the cat?"

"No."

"You are a killer."

"I have heard that and read accounts of it, but I have no memory of it."

Karissa stared at him, wondering what it would be like to lead the life allotted to Asheris in which he lost every night to the ruthless nature of a big cat.

"That is why I tried to locate you for so many years, Karissa. I believe that you are the key to finding Senefret and ending this accursed life of mine."

The mention of Senefret brought back her heartache in full force. She looked down to hide the hurt in her eyes from him.

"You should have told me the truth right from the start," she remarked. It required great effort to keep her voice from cracking in anguish.

"You would not have understood. You would have been afraid of me." He kissed the tips of her fingers and slipped out of the bed. "But you are not afraid of me now, are you?"

She shook her head, knowing things would be simpler if he didn't treat her with such warmth and kindness. It broke her heart to think that he had pledged his love to someone else.

"But it wasn't fair of you to lead me on."

"Lead you on?"

"Yes." She glanced up at him, knowing her gaze was full of recrimination. "You led me to believe you cared for me when all along you saw Senefret every time you looked at me."

"That is not true."

"Then why did you give me her dresses to wear, her jewelry to put around my neck?"

"Because when I look at you, Karissa, you are everything I remember from the days I was a whole man. The modern world falls away when I am with you. I can forget the centuries of loneliness when you are in my arms. There is something about you that calls to me, deep inside in a place that has no voice—no words to explain—only feelings that cry out to be heard. Yes, you remind me of Senefret, but that is only the barest beginning of what I see in you."

"I don't believe you!" She jumped to her feet. She realized she was crying. His words had moved her, but she still couldn't trust him. Karissa swiped at her wet cheeks. "You are obsessed with her!"

"I search for her out of love and honor, Karissa. I must assure Senefret a proper journey to her afterlife. I could have done much more for her had I gone back to Thebes in time. I might have saved her life. But I chased after my own glory. And I soon discovered that glory is meaningless, empty, nothing." He sighed bitterly. "I had to learn my lesson about the importance of love by losing the only woman I had ever cared for."

"And you still love her, don't you?"

"Yes, I love her—the memory of her. When you truly love someone, it is forever."

"I see." Karissa reached for her cotton pants and pulled them on, stuffing the khaki shirt in the waistband. She felt as if she would shatter into a thousand pieces of despair if he said anything else about his priestess. The sooner she got him out of the hotel and into a cab, the sooner she could get him out of her life and begin the long battle to forget him.

He stepped up behind her. "Why must you be upset?" he asked.

"I'm not upset. I'm simply in a hurry. We don't want anyone coming up here and asking questions, do we?"

"No."

"So, hang on and I'll get you something to wear."

Asheris regarded her for a long moment as if he wanted to say more, but then seemed to think better of it. He reached for the bourbon. Karissa hurried to the door that connected her room with Josh's and slid back the dead bolt. She turned the knob, hoping that Josh hadn't bolted the door from his side. He hadn't. The latch clicked open, and she swept into the room.

Asheris was taller and more slender than Josh, but Josh's clothes would do in a pinch. She grabbed a pair of jeans, sandals, and a shirt out of his messy suitcase and returned to the room.

"Here," she said, handing them to Asheris, "I'll tell Josh that we borrowed these."

"I do not think you understand all that I have said."

"Oh, I understand." She brushed back her hair in a brisk gesture, trying to affect a casual air. "I respect you for keeping your vows, I really do. But from now on, just leave me out of your obsessions, okay?"

He frowned slightly and then sighed, as if he had abandoned the effort to reason with her. Then he untied the robe. It fell to the floor before Karissa could turn around. Didn't he care that she would see him naked?

She headed for the door while he pulled on the clothes. "Hurry, Asheris. Josh is bound to return any minute." She turned to see if he were dressed.

"I am ready." He looked up.

For a moment Karissa gazed at him dressed in Josh's blue and white striped shirt tucked into a pair of blue jeans. Asheris' lean frame lent the clothes a neatly tailored look, completely different than the way Josh appeared in them. Asheris was the type of man who would look well-groomed in anything, but she knew it had more to do with the carriage of the man inside the clothing than the clothing itself.

They took the elevator to the lobby. On the way down, Asheris sank against the back of the car and closed his eyes.

"Are you all right?" Karissa asked, watching the color fade from his face.

"Only light-headed," he replied.

"You lost a lot of blood out there in the garden," she said. "Here, put your arm around me. I'll help you keep to your feet until you get to the cab."

Asheris seemed grateful to drape his arm around her shoulders. "If I use you as a support, will not people think there is something amiss?" he asked.

"No. They'll probably think we're just crazy about each other."

"Are we not, Karissa?" he asked quietly, looking down at her with his smoldering golden eyes. "Do you not understand what it is I feel for you?"

She shook her head slowly, mesmerized by the heat in his eyes.

"You are a part of me," he said. "Your eyes speak to my heart."

Before she could say anything, he bent down to kiss her, his breath faintly laced with bourbon. His lips and his words drove a shaft deep into the core of her and pierced through the armor she had been wearing as protection against his charm and kindness. In the face of his confession, her armor fell away, leaving her emotions more raw than ever. She reached up to touch his cheek as her heart surged in her chest. The elevator dipped to a stop. Only the sound of the doors whisking open kept her from turning in his arms and revealing how she felt about him.

She was yanked back to reality by the sound of a familiar voice.

"Karissa! What in the world?"

Karissa pulled away from Asheris' mouth to see Josh standing in the lobby with a stunned look on his face. She straightened, and Asheris let his arm slide away.

Josh stared at them, from one to the other, as Karissa and Asheris stepped out of the elevator.

"Karissa?" he asked, his voice cracking. "What's going on? What's Asher doing here?"

"Mr. Asher has a discovery to show me," she said. "We're going to the desert for a couple of hours."

"But—what about our flight?"

"I don't know, Josh."

"But..." Josh moved to the side as Karissa brushed past him. "Wait a minute, he's wearing my clothes."

"I'll bring them back, Josh."

"You'll bring them back?" Josh exclaimed. "What in the hell is going on?"

Karissa saw a few hotel patrons and the desk clerk turn their heads and look at them. "Please, Josh, keep your voice down."

"Okay, but..." Josh sputtered as he followed them toward the front door of the lobby. "...but Karissa, you can't go like this. We're flying home together in a few hours. I came all this way just for you!"

"I know, and I appreciate it, Josh, but I can't go back right now."

"What about the PBS interview?"

"I'll be there in time."

"But I thought you and I..." He broke off and glanced at Asheris and then back to her. "I always thought we—aw, the hell with it!"

He came to a complete stop at the door of the hotel, as if the truth had suddenly dawned on him. Karissa glanced at him and could hardly bear to look at the crestfallen expression on his face.

"It would be best if you went back to Baltimore," she said gently. "Really, Josh."

"Karissa is safe with me," Asheris put in kindly. "Though you cannot see it now, Mr. Lambert."

"I can't believe it, Karissa. You've always given the cold shoulder to every man you've ever met. Why not this guy? What's so fucking special about him?"

"I'll explain when I get back," Karissa said, pushing open the door. "But right now, we've got to run. Good-bye, Josh."

"See you in Baltimore," he replied in a resigned tone.

Relieved that Josh had accepted the situation, she followed Asheris through the doorway and out to the sidewalk where a taxi waited at the curb.

By the time they tended to Asheris' wound, ate a light meal, and drove out to the site of the sphinx, the afternoon sun was already well on its way toward the horizon and the desert was an inferno. Karissa drove the Land Rover to spare Asheris the pain of shifting, and by the time they arrived at their desert destination, his high coloring had returned, and he appeared to have more energy. Karissa was relieved that he was recovering so swiftly from his loss of blood. By the time they reached the rock formation, he claimed to feel much better, except for the soreness in his shoulder.

They got out of the truck and Asheris led her to the site where laborers had cleared away an impressive amount of sand to reveal a jumble of pink granite blocks. In the pile was a dark hole as tall as a man. Karissa shaded her eyes and peered in the direction of the opening.

"A passageway," Asheris remarked. "Come, I will show you."

They hurried toward the twenty or so men who were streaming in and out of the passage carrying buckets of sand and dumping them a few yards away. A single man in long flowing robes and turban stood near the entry with a rifle cradled in his arms. When he caught sight of Asheris, he strode up to them.

"Mr. Asher," he greeted with a huge grin and then flashed an interested glance at Karissa. "We have found something!"

"What, Jamal?"

"A sealed room. We have been waiting for hours for you to come and see."

"I was detained." Asheris took Karissa's elbow. "Let us have a look."

"We cannot show you now."

"Why not?"

"It is too late." Jamal glanced around fearfully. "You know the men will not stay here after sundown because of Lord Azhur."

"I told you not to worry about Lord Azhur. He is only a character in a legend."

"The men will not stay. No matter what you pay them, it will not be done."

Karissa glanced at Asheris, wondering what he would do. Already the men had stopped working and were piling their tools in a rusting, battered old lorry while others climbed in the back.

He squeezed Karissa's elbow. "We'll find the room ourselves. Is there a lantern in the sphinx?"

"Assuredly. Five of them, sir. Keep to the corridor and go to the right. You will find the sealed room. No problem."

"Thank you." Asheris frowned. "Has there been any trouble with Mustofa or his men?"

"No, Mr. Asher. They do not see us working on this side of the dune. We are discreet, as you have instructed."

"Good. Then I will see you tomorrow."

"Tomorrow then, sir, at dawn as you wish." Jamal gave a quick bow and then hurried toward the truck, which was already idling. The men motioned for Jamal to hurry.

"Come," Asheris said. "Let us see what we can find."

Karissa surveyed the jumble of blocks, remembering in vivid detail the way the sphinx had collapsed upon itself many years ago. "Is it safe?"

"Once we get in the corridor, we will be out of danger. The temple was solidly built. Only the booby-traps collapsed. You will see."

Asheris led her forward.

By the time they turned right into the long corridor, Asheris' heart thudded in his chest, not from the effort of walking, but from anticipation. After centuries of separation and grief, he might be meters away from Senefret. He held the lantern aloft and grimaced from the pain that shot through his left shoulder.

"There's the sealed doorway," he said, almost in a whisper.

Karissa clutched his upper arm and drew close to him. Even though he didn't wish for her to be frightened, he loved the way she clung to him in the dark, as if she depended upon him to keep her safe. He would give his life to protect her and wished she would believe his feelings for her were genuine.

"What do the seals say?" she asked, releasing his arm to reach out and touch the ancient plaster of the arid subterranean chamber. The walls were preserved so well they still looked freshly painted in reds and ochres and black.

Asheris stepped forward and craned his neck to see the hieroglyphs stamped in the plaster. His heart skipped a beat as he glimpsed the familiar group of glyphs surrounded by an oval line that made up the cartouche, or symbol, of Senefret's name.

"It is her name. She is here!" he said. The raspy sound of his voice echoed in the darkness. "This is Senefret's tomb."

Karissa squeezed his arm, happy to share his excitement.

Then Asheris noticed the way the plaster was roughly applied and the crooked placement of some of the seals. He bent down and inspected the wall.

"What's the matter?" Karissa asked, noticing his disquiet.

"This door has been sealed twice, Karissa. Someone entered the tomb after the burial and sealed it up again." He touched a crooked seal. "The second seal was done in haste."

"Do you think grave robbers might have plundered the tomb already?"

"Thieves would not take the time to reseal the chamber." He put the lantern on the dusty floor. "Give me the crowbar, and I will get started."

Feverishly, he chipped away each seal until a rectangular line revealed the entrance to the tomb. All the while he worked, he wondered why someone had gone into the tomb after the burial. What would he find? Most of all he worried that someone might have burned Senefret's mummified body, thus eliminating the possibility of an afterlife for her. He couldn't bear the thought.

Like a madman he hacked away at the blocks, pulverizing the old plaster and limestone. He had to know. He had to find her. With every stroke, he prayed to the gods that he would discover Senefret's mummy unmolested. He didn't care about the treasures with which she might have been buried. His only concern was to find her body.

After what seemed like hours, he loosened a block enough to push it into the chamber. It thudded to the floor on the other side. The air of the room beyond drifted past them, still fragrant with myrrh and cedar. Karissa stood near him, holding the lantern up to help him see his progress. Shortly afterward he knocked another block free. After that there was a quick succession of loose blocks, which afforded an opening big enough to crouch through. He ducked into the opening. His shoulder burned and throbbed from the exertion, but he refused to give in to the pain.

"Come!" he exclaimed, too excited to remember proper English. "The lantern to me, please!"

Karissa relinquished the light and dipped into the chamber after him.

Once in the burial chamber, Asheris rose to his feet and grabbed her elbow to help her stand. They both took in the sight of the tomb as they stood hand in hand in a pool of light.

In the center of the small room lay a stone sarcophagus covered with hieroglyphics, on the top of which was a small cedar box, the size of a paperback novel. Asheris stared at the sarcophagus, stuck dumb with emotion. Here lay the love of his life. All that remained of her.

He had known death on the battlefield. He had known the death of his parents from fever. But none of those passings had affected him as much as the sight of Senefret's grave.

"Where are all her things?" Karissa asked. "Her furniture, her belongings?"

Asheris blinked away his grief and looked around at the bare floor, strewn with dried flower blossoms and wreaths.

"She died in disgrace. Perhaps the priestesses forbid her to be buried with anything that might help her in the afterlife."

"Could grave robbers have taken everything?"

Asheris considered the question and then shook his head. "No. See? The flowers have remained undisturbed except for that single path from the sarcophagus to the door. As you can see, no one has walked anywhere else in the chamber."

"So, what's in the little box?"

"We shall see," Asheris replied, stepping toward the sarcophagus. "And then we will find out if Senefret is here with us."

He picked up the cedar box just as running footsteps echoed in the corridor outside. Alarmed, Karissa grabbed his arm. Asheris reached for the crowbar and thrust the box into her hand just as a gun and a man's arm appeared in the opening of the tomb.

Chapter Nine

"I will kill whoever moves first," barked a voice in the darkness.

Hoping no one could see her, Karissa slipped the cedar box into her shirt. Asheris held the crowbar in the air, ready to strike, although they both knew that it would be little defense against a gun.

The armed man motioned for someone to crawl into the chamber. Two other men stepped through. Asheris made a move to accost them, but the man with the gun shouted, "I will shoot Miss Spencer if you so much as strike one of my men."

Karissa recognized the voice of Mustofa.

With an exasperated sigh, Asheris moved back to protect Karissa with his body, while Mustofa crawled into the chamber and straightened. The lantern threw shadows on his gaunt face, accentuating the hollows of his cheeks and his cold deep-set eyes. He smiled.

"This tomb seems rather barren," Mustofa continued, sweeping the air with his hand. "But I am sure there are others, are there not?"

"The others should not be disturbed, Mustofa," Asheris warned. "There is a reason this place is called the Valley of the Damned."

"A ruse, surely," Mustofa sneered. "To deter those of us who seek the treasure buried here."

"It is no ruse."

"Then what are you doing here?"

"A matter of personal honor, something I do not expect you to understand."

Mustofa narrowed his eyes. For a moment he studied Asheris, and then he shifted his regard to Karissa. She kept her expression as blank as possible, all the while praying he wouldn't notice the box in her shirt. His sneer pulled his mouth to one side.

"Tie them up, Rashad," he ordered. "Ali, get the lid off this coffin."

A short squat man strode forward, slipping a coil of rope off his shoulder.

"No tricks, Asher," warned Mustofa. "Or Miss Spencer will be punished. Do you understand?"

"I understand."

"Then put down the crowbar," Mustofa said.

Asheris dropped the tool. The metallic clank echoed through the old temple and disappeared far in the distance. Rashad kicked the tool across the room, well out of range. Then Rashad stepped behind them and yanked Karissa's arms behind her. The cedar box dug into the tender flesh of her belly, but she made no sound. He lashed the rough rope around her wrists and pushed her down on the floor where he tied her ankles as well. He did the same to Asheris.

Meanwhile Mustofa and Ali had managed to slide the heavy stone lid to one side so the contents of the vault could be viewed. Mustofa stepped closer to see inside. He picked up the lantern and held it near his head.

Karissa watched him, knowing from her father's lessons that Mustofa was probably looking at a wooden sarcophagus.

Many nobles and kings were buried within three sarcophagi—stone, wood and lastly solid gold. She found herself holding her breath as the other men gaped at the contents of the coffin.

"Let us get the other lid off and we will see if this is worth our trouble." Mustofa held the lantern high as his man pried off the wooden lid of the second coffin. Once he got it loose, he heaved it over the side as if it had no value, even though it was covered with intricate paintings and inlaid with semiprecious stones. She knew what they were interested in—the gold layer.

Mustofa gazed upon the treasure of the inner sarcophagus, and his eyes lit up with delight and greed.

"Ah, look at that beauty!" he exclaimed. "We are rich!"

Karissa exchanged a look of frustration with Asheris. He yanked at the ropes that bound him, but he couldn't pull free.

Mustofa looked over at him. "You might as well accept your fate, Mr. Asher. You are not going anywhere. I cannot allow you to get in my way, not when a fortune is to be found here."

"Do not disturb the evil ones buried here, Mustofa!" Asheris warned. "You will unleash those better left entombed."

"Superstition and lies, Asher. I do not believe you for a moment! You want it all for your precious museums!"

Asheris scowled and glared at the flower-strewn floor of the tomb. There was no use arguing with a greedy man like Mustofa.

"Rashad," Mustofa ordered. "You will remain outside the tomb to make sure Mr. Asher and Miss Spencer stay where they are. Ali, you come with me. We must go back to Luxor for crates and weapons before Asher's men return in the morning."

"Yes, boss."

"We will be back at dawn, Asher," Mustofa commented, stuffing his pistol in his belt. "Sleep well."

Then with a dry laugh, Mustofa took the lantern and left them tied up in complete darkness. The gloom was so intense that Karissa couldn't see her feet in front of her. A sheen of sweat broke out on the surface of her skin. She was deep in the earth near the ruins of the haunted sphinx, at the feet of a dead priestess, and very close to the place where the stone had crushed her father. How could she survive the coming hours without losing her mind? Would she perish in the same place as her father, with no one knowing what had happened to her?

"Asheris?" she called through the blackness. Her voice quavered. She scooted closer to him but stopped in surprise when she heard the low growl of a panther.

"Asheris?" she called again. Had he transformed in the darkness and freed himself of the rope? She couldn't see a thing!

She heard a low growl vibrate in the gloom.

Then something soft and velvety brushed her cheek. His tail? Karissa held herself stiff, wondering what the panther would do to her. She felt a warm shoulder rub gently against hers and then the cat stretched out along the side of her leg. In the stillness of the tomb, she heard the quiet thrum of his purr and felt the rise and fall of his powerful rib cage against her knee. For a long while she held her breath, not daring to move, until she realized the panther was standing guard over her. Gradually her tense muscles relaxed, and she resigned herself to spending the night in the bowels of the earth with her strange otherworldly companion.

Hours later she awakened to the sound of a man's terrified scream. Karissa jerked to attention, unable to tell what time of day it was or what was happening. All was still completely black. The cat was no longer lying beside her. Desperately she peered into the blackness, trying to make out something—anything—in the gloom. She heard a slow dragging sound go past the doorway of the tomb. And then all was quiet again. She struggled against her bonds to sit up, grimacing in pain at the cramps in her hips and shoulders and waited in the oppressive silence for Lord Azhur to return.

After what seemed like hours, she saw a light pass by the tomb entrance and then the light came through the opening in the blocks. Karissa watched anxiously and was relieved to see Asheris duck into the chamber. He glanced at her and slid the lantern toward her.

"Are you all right?" he asked.

"Yes." She tried to focus on his face, because he was completely naked again, and it was a shock to see him unclothed. "What about the guard, Rashad?"

"He's dead."

She didn't ask anything more about Rashad's death. She could guess what had happened to him.

Asheris stepped behind her and knelt down to untie her bonds. When he was finished, he pressed a quick kiss just below her left ear. "We must hurry," he said. "Dawn has come and Mustofa and his men will be back any moment."

Karissa struggled to her feet and rolled her shoulders as Asheris slipped into his clothes. She minced to the sarcophagus on stiff legs and looked into the stone coffin. Inside was the golden inner coffin, still as luminous as the day Senefret had been interred. The funerary mask showed a lovely face with large eyes and a sensitive mouth. If the mask bore a likeness to the young priestess, she must have been very beautiful. No wonder Asheris had fallen in love with her.

Asheris came up behind her. "Help me lift the lid," he said, striding to the foot of the coffin.

Karissa reached down and felt with her fingertips for the lip of the cover. After a few minutes of prying and swearing, they managed to free the top. Though the cover was a thin shell, it was astoundingly heavy, having been covered with pure gold.

"It's too heavy!" Karissa gasped.

"Slide it your way then," Asheris said, straining with the effort of supporting most of the weight. Karissa staggered back a few steps, just enough to tilt the golden lid against the edge of the thick wall of the outer stone sarcophagus.

"Good," Asheris panted, carefully lowering his end. "I can reach inside. That is all that matters."

He stooped and grabbed the lantern, and then bent closer for a better look. Karissa moved to his elbow and peered in. She could see a linen-wrapped figure. A sweet musky smell rose up from the mummy. Dried flowers littered the body and the inside of the coffin.

For a moment Asheris stood there, simply staring down at the mummy, as if caught in his dreams. Gently Karissa touched his elbow.

"Is it Senefret?" she asked.

"It is her likeness on the coffin."

"She was very beautiful."

"Yes." He turned and held out the lantern. "Take the lantern and turn the wooden lid flat on the floor. We will use it to carry Senefret out of her tomb."

Karissa hurried to do his bidding and didn't question his directions, for she knew it would be impossible for them to drag the golden coffin out of the chamber, no matter how precious it was to Senefret's afterlife.

Reverently, Asheris lifted the mummy out of the half open coffin and carried it to the wooden lid. Gently he deposited the wrapped bundle onto the lid and then looked up.

"We will slide the lid out to the hallway. Then we can pick it up. It should not be too heavy."

"Sounds like a plan." Karissa wiped her palms on her cotton pants. The notion of walking around in a tomb with a dead person's body made her break into a sweat all over again. "What will we do if Mustofa comes before we get out of the sphinx?"

"We will try to find a place of concealment along the way. Give the lantern to me and I will hang it on my arm."

She held the light out to him and then squatted down to push the lid along the floor. The small cedar box scraped against her ribs. In all the excitement, she had forgotten about it. Still, it would have to wait until they were out of danger.

The scraping sound of wood against limestone echoed through the corridor and made Karissa even more nervous. She was certain that someone or something would hear the racket. Hours seemed to pass before they hoisted the lid into the air and carried it down the shadowed hall. Karissa took up the rear because it was easier walking forward than backward, the way Asheris was walking. The only drawback to the rear position was knowing her back was vulnerable to the unholy inhabitants of the Valley of the Damned. Her heart thudded in her chest, making her light-headed and short of breath. She kept her eyes and thoughts focused on the faint patch of light in the distance.

Just as they passed through the jumbled blocks of the demolished sphinx, Asheris lurched to a stop.

"What?" Karissa whispered.

"I heard an engine," he replied. "Someone is coming!"

Asheris glanced around quickly to locate a place to hide. Then he propped the edge of the coffin lid on one knee and used his right hand to turn off the lantern. She felt a tug on the wood as he guided her around a pile of blocks and into a closet-sized opening. Karissa scraped her shoulder on a piece of granite but stifled the cry that formed in her throat.

They watched in heart-stopping dread as Mustofa and his men tramped through the ruins carrying shovels, picks, and crates, ready to plunder as much as they could before Asheris' crew arrived for the day. Then they'd most likely kill Jamal and his men or run them off.

As soon as the others had turned the corner toward Senefret's tomb, Asheris moved out of the little hiding spot and pulled her toward the opening in the sphinx. They practically trotted, and Karissa worried with every step that the mummy would bounce off its unseemly bier.

The cold light of morning nearly blinded her. Her eyes watered and she sneezed as they stumbled onto the sand. Walking up the slope of the dune became a strenuous exercise as the sand gave way with each step they took. Karissa glanced over her shoulder, praying that Mustofa's men would not come after them. She couldn't remember feeling as desperate in her entire life.

Just as they reached the Land Rover, Karissa heard a metallic click deep in the earth, and then a resounding thud. Even from a distance the noise was quite loud. Memories from the past rushed back in a hot flood as she heard the horrible and far-too-familiar sound of a giant block of stone sliding down a track.

She whipped around to say something, but Asheris held up his hand to stop her, his head cocked as he listened intently.

Then from deep inside the sphinx came a sound like the collision of two locomotives. Blocks of granite rolled out of the sand and bounced down to the bottom of the dune. The entrance to the sphinx disappeared in a shower of granite and sand. Someone screamed and the cry pierced through the thunder of the cave-in and then was gone. As if to answer the dead man, a sharp wind came whistling across the dune, blasting sand into Karissa's face and blinding her to the murderous landscape below. She hunched away from the biting wind. "The sphinx is falling apart!" she cried.

"We must hurry! The whole area might give way."

Asheris threw open the back doors of the Land Rover and motioned for her to jump in. He hoisted the lid and the mummy into the back of the vehicle, slammed the doors, and ran around to the driver's side. Karissa knelt in the cargo hold to secure the mummy and then pulled the cedar box out of her shirt and put it on the floor beside Senefret's body. When she was sure the mummy wouldn't budge, she climbed over the back seat to the front just as Asheris pulled away from the rock formation and headed for the road.

Karissa fell into the passenger seat and looked back to see the dune sliding into a gigantic pit. Blocks of granite rolled into the pit, bouncing end over end as if sucked into a whirlpool of sand. Soon the wind became so fierce and full of sand that she couldn't see beyond the rock formation.

Pale and stricken, she turned to Asheris. "What do you think happened?" she asked, brushing the gritty hair out of her eyes.

"Mustofa must have tried carrying the golden sarcophagus out of the tomb. And his greed outweighed his caution."

"He set off a booby-trap."

"Very likely."

"Why didn't we set it off?"

"Some traps are fashioned to spring when a certain weight passes across a portion of the floor. We took nothing but the body of a woman—feather light after her long sleep in the desert."

"Do you think they're all dead?"

"Yes."

Karissa regarded Asheris' sharp profile and the sad turn to his sensual mouth. He had found his long-lost love and was about to give her over to the afterlife. He had nearly completed his task. So why wasn't he relieved that his work was almost done? He seemed more troubled than ever.

"What's wrong, Asheris?" she asked.

He reached over and placed his hand on her thigh. "I must think for a while, my sweet." Then he slid his hand away and glanced at her, but the usual warmth in his eyes was gone. In its place was a weariness and concern she had never seen before. She longed to ease his trouble, but realized she might help him most by honoring his request for silence. She sat back and closed her eyes, bone weary herself.

Six hours later, Karissa stood in a private guest cabin aboard the freighter Victoria, in quarters Asheris had booked for a trip down the Nile. Outside a windstorm raged, as if the gale had followed Senefret's body from tomb to river.

Karissa rubbed her arms and thought about Asheris while the ship rocked beneath her. He had gone below to make sure Senefret's crate was stowed securely. He was due back any moment. She wondered what she should say to Asheris in regard to her feelings for him. She couldn't imagine going back to Baltimore without telling him how much she cared for him. And yet if she did disclose her feelings, what good could come of it? She and Asheris were soon to return to their usual lives. Revealing her feelings would only complicate a smooth re-entry. And yet she longed for him to open his soul to her as he had once compelled her to open to him.

Asheris had spent the morning procuring a coffin and a crate for the transport of Senefret's body, and getting tickets for a ship to take them down the Nile to a suitable burial site with which he was acquainted. He had convinced Karissa that it would be safer for her to accompany him and then be escorted to the airport the next day. Mustofa might have miraculously survived the cave-in and decided to come after them to keep them quiet about the treasure trove in the Valley of the Damned.

Karissa had agreed to his plan. If she flew out by tomorrow, she could still make the PBS interview, although once she got to Baltimore, she would hardly have time to take a breath before the film crew arrived at her studio. But she knew she didn't want to leave Asheris until the last moment. She might never see him again. Every minute between now and tomorrow morning would be precious, even though Asheris had lapsed into a contemplative mood that shut her out and worried her.

She heard the key in the lock and slowly turned to face him.

He came into the cabin, glanced at her and smiled, and then carefully shut the door.

"Is everything all right?" she asked.

"Yes." He ran both hands through his hair. "Now we can relax for a few hours."

He let his arms fall to his sides and walked to the couch where he sank down and stretched his arms along the back of the cushions. He was dressed in tan cotton pants and a tan and white striped shirt with the sleeves rolled up as usual. When she looked at him, however, all she could see was his naked torso and the light dusting of black hair on his chest. She blinked away the vision and lifted her gaze to his face. He was studying her.

"How is your shoulder?" she asked.

"It will heal in time."

"Time." She sighed and sat in a chair next to the couch. "Everything has to do with time, doesn't it? I feel like a slave to it, especially now."

"I have been thinking about time all day," he said, "and how fickle it can be."

"And why is that?"

"Because of you."

She flushed with the pleasure at hearing him echo her own thoughts. "Because my time in Egypt is almost gone?"

"It is more complicated than that."

Karissa looked down at her hands. Why did she think he was going to talk about Senefret again? If he mentioned her once more, she'd have to leave the room because she wouldn't be able to hold back her tears. She longed to be the woman foremost in his heart and mind—in fact, the only woman in his life. And when he spoke of loving Senefret, he unknowingly caused her sorrow.

She felt his touch on her hand as he linked her fingers in his, always making a connection with her. Asheris' rich voice rumbled softly. "In all the years I spent searching for a lost part of my life, I felt adrift. I believed I felt adrift because I was separated from Senefret."

That damned Senefret.

Karissa felt a lump forming in her throat and tried to pull away, but he wouldn't release her. She jumped to her feet.

"Let me go," she said, pulling her hand from his. "Talking about Senefret is the last thing I want to do."

"Wait, Karissa." He stood up and took her shoulders. "You must hear me out this one last time."

She swallowed her anguish and stood there, loving the weight of his hands on her shoulders. He looked down and his dark lashes swept his cheeks. "You are not aware of all the feelings I possess. Senefret is with me now, on her way to her rightful resting place. I should spend the day praying for her reunited soul, her *akh*. And yet," he paused and raised his glance to look at her. "At the same time, I am reminded that the hours with you, Karissa, are quickly coming to an end."

Was he saying that he might choose a real woman over an ancient memory wrapped in gauze?

"I have been struggling with this for days," he added. "My head keeps reminding me of my duty to Senefret, but my heart is telling me to consider something entirely different."

"And what is that?" she asked, praying he would say the words she longed to hear, that he loved her and that she was more important to him than the dead priestess. "What is your heart saying?"

"That I should spend these hours with you."

She touched his cheek. "What would be so wrong with that?"

"It would show disrespect of Senefret. And unfairness to you. I do not even know where my own heart lies, Karissa, and yet I wish for you to give yourself to me."

"And if I give myself freely? No strings attached?"

"It would still be unfair. I am not a whole man, Karissa, neither in heart nor in body, as you well know. I can offer only a part of myself."

"Then I will accept whatever you give me," she replied.

The pressure of his hands increased. "How can that be enough for you?"

"Because you will be more special to me than any other man."

"How can you be sure?"

"Because..." She stroked his temple and pushed her fingertips into his lustrous black hair. "Because I love you, Asheris." The words she thought would be difficult to say burst from her lips with surprising ease and warmth born of the truth in her heart. "Even if you don't love me in return, it still won't change the way I feel. I have fallen in love with you. I can't deny it."

He stared at her, a strange light in his eyes, as if her words had paralyzed him. Then she raised up on tiptoe and pressed her lips against his. The instant their mouths met, she felt a melting sensation, a surrender in her body as well as in his. With a low moan, Asheris' hands slid down to her elbows as he bent to the kiss, and her hands slid up the front of his shirt and around his neck. The fragrance of his shampoo, his clean shirt, and his faint scent of coriander filled her senses as his tongue slipped into her mouth. She closed her eyes tightly, embracing him with all her heart as his hands moved up and down her back and into her hair. For a long, lingering moment the only sound in the cabin was the rush of their breathing and the brush of his palms on her blouse.

How could his heart not be in his caress, his kiss? No one could be as passionate as Asheris without possessing deep feelings to fire such embraces. He simply couldn't recognize that he loved her just as fiercely as she loved him.

"Asheris," she whispered, her skin tingling as he kissed her neck. Her body was crying out for his touch and for the feel of his naked skin against hers. She reached for the buttons of his crisp shirt.

"If we start this, I will not wish to stop," he said, his voice husky. "It is not my desire to hold back."

"No one is asking you to hold back."

She looked into his face and saw Asheris' mouth slanting upward in his dazzling, slow smile.

Chapter Ten

Karissa pulled his shirt out of his pants and caressed his torso as a faint growl rolled up his throat. She slipped the shirt off his shoulders and down his arms. It fell on the floor behind him. Then she pressed a kiss in the center of his chest and hugged him, filling her soul with the glory of his warm being against her cheek and the pounding of his heart in her ear. This was what she wanted more than anything in the world—to make love with Asheris, to hold him in her arms, to cherish him.

He eased her back, unbuttoned her blouse, and drew if off. He kissed her and unhooked the fastener of her bra. This, too, he lifted away to release her breasts. She looked up to see his face was flushed.

"You are beautiful," he whispered in awe, and he kissed her between her breasts, just as she had done to him.

Her nipples hardened with desire. She closed her eyes and sighed with pleasure as his golden hands swept down from her shoulders, and the pads of his hands passed over the firm peaks of her breasts.

"Asheris!" she gasped.

As if to torment her, he captured her left breast in his hand and surrounded her right nipple with his mouth. He licked her, lightly at first, until she plunged her hands into his hair to draw him closer. She wanted him to consume her breast, to take her into him as she wanted to take him into her body. Soon he was pulling on her nipple, half sucking and half biting, and she arched back to allow him more room, while short cries of pleasure burst from her lips.

Asheris tipped her into his arms, sweeping her off the ground. As he carried her to the bedroom, she clung to him and rolled her head onto his hot bare chest, highly aware of the way her hips brushed across the front of his trousers with every step he took.

He laid her down on the coverlet, and she sank back against the pillows. Asheris stood there gazing at her as he unbuckled his belt. She returned his regard and reached for the button on her waistband, but he stopped her so he could be the one to unfasten it. Then he unzipped her pants and slowly dragged them off. Next came her underclothes, and she was naked.

With a few quick movements, he stripped. His manhood jutted out, swollen and magnificent, and she felt a powerful stirring inside at the sight of him. When he knelt on the bed and straddled her, she reached out and stroked him, anxious to touch his hardened, silken flesh.

"Ah!" he said, gritting his teeth.

"You are beautiful, too," she gasped, cupping the rest of his sensitive flesh.

"You are the beautiful one," he declared, kissing her. He lowered his torso until his chest grazed her nipples and his shaft brushed her belly. He moved upward slightly, just enough to create an erotic friction between them. She moaned in his mouth.

He eased her legs open and moved in between them, never once freeing her mouth. Her hands swept over his back and down his arms as she arched upward. With each brush of his body, she felt a throbbing ache blossoming deep within her. Nothing had prepared her for the hunger she felt for this man. When she shifted to get closer to him, he moved his hips forward, and his shaft came up against her. They both let out a ragged sigh.

Then as if he already knew the landscape of her body, he found her entrance in a single stroke. Karissa shivered in ecstasy as he eased into her. She clasped the backs of his arms and sank into the coverlet, surrendering to him. He pushed farther inside her, filling her with his hard bluntness, and she smiled with joy at the sensation of taking him in. She had never wanted a man more, never wanted to be filled like this, never felt such profound rightness in lying beneath a man and accepting him. And she had never, ever had this urge to grin.

Asheris kissed her smile. "You like this, yes?"

"Oh, yes!"

"It is beyond imagining."

"Yes." She ran her hands down his back as he plunged deeper and deeper inside her, until he pulled back with exquisite control.

"Please, Asheris," she whispered. "Don't stop."

"You want all of me, then?"

She knew exactly what he meant. He wanted to pour himself into her but didn't know if she would accept that. The truth was, she longed for his essence to flood into her. It was a startling realization. She loved Asheris as she had never loved anyone. She wanted everything of him.

Karissa took his face in her hands and looked him in the eyes. "Yes, I want you," she said, "all of you."

Her words sent him into a frenzy. He plunged into her, rocking her until her breasts were bouncing between them and his skin was wet with sweat, and she was grabbing his buttocks and writhing beneath him, chanting his name over and over again, and his seed was bursting out in a glorious rush, filling her, and she was wrapped around his body and wrapped around his manhood, squeezing him until he was spent and trembling and collapsing upon her. She lay there rigid beneath him, grabbing the bedspread on either side as her body was racked by wave after wave of orgasm, pressing down on him, pushing him out.

Almost as soon as she sank back, breathless and shuddering, Asheris felt himself growing hard again. He had never recovered so quickly with a woman. Giving her a few moments to catch her breath, Asheris kissed her breasts, her neck, and then her parted lips. Her eyes opened halfway as she regarded him with a sultry, sated expression that sent shafts of joy through him and made him plunge anew inside her.

This time, her orgasm vaulted her far beyond anything he had ever witnessed. She cried out, clutching at him, clawing at him, her eyes rolled back, her jaw thrust upward, half-human, half-animal, her body quaking. She looked as if she were traveling through space. Through time. Through a wonderland only she could traverse.

When she finally collapsed into the bedsheets, spent, her eyes fluttered open. For a long moment she gazed deeply into his eyes, a half-smile on her lips. He could feel a similar smile on his own.

"And how would you do this if you were a panther?" she asked, raising one eyebrow as if teasing him. Her question inflamed him, for he had fantasized about that very thing.

He paused for a moment, weighing the possibility that he might alarm her with the truth. But somehow, he knew that Karissa would not be afraid of anything he did with her. He slipped out of her and grabbed her wrists.

He saw the look of surprise in her eyes as he twisted her onto her stomach. With a few more nudges, he urged her onto her knees and elbows. Then he took her, his chest riding her back, his hands clutching her breasts, his body slamming against her sweet pale rump, his every thrust rocking her forward. She sank her forehead into the pillow and grabbed the edges of the pillowcase. He could see her knuckles growing white as he found his rhythm. This time he seemed to last forever, even through her cries of release. Then what began as a climax for him transformed into a state of oblivion, into a timeless coming, of a shattering, shimmering joining that went on and on and on. He heard his voice uttering a growling noise, and then he closed his teeth upon the flesh at the base of her beautiful neck as he let himself go inside her in a flood. He emptied himself completely, exquisitely, and utterly.

For a moment they hung there together unmoving, as if neither of them could believe what had just passed between them. Asheris let out a long sigh and raised his head. Slowly Karissa melted onto the coverlet, and he melted with her, both of them slick with sweat and seed. He kissed her hot cheek, stroked her outstretched arms, and then eased his body away. She moved her arm to allow him room, and Asheris lay down beside her, his leg across her calves, while both of them struggled to catch their breath.

As the wind rocked the ship, Asheris relaxed and spread his hand across her flank. He liked the way his hand looked on her, possessing her like that. His manhood had burst twice inside her, and the experience had been phenomenal. But as he lay there, he felt his heart bursting with love for her, and the feeling overwhelmed him.

He loved this woman. He loved her beyond anything he had ever known. And he longed to reveal his feelings. But how fair would it be if he declared his love knowing full well that he might never be able to give his heart completely.

He hadn't known until this moment that he could not settle for less. He wanted everything with Karissa. Giving parts of himself would never be enough, not for him and not for her. It would have to be all or nothing, even if it meant never making love with her again. Anything less would be too frustrating, too painful.

Desperate with anguish and despair, he gathered Karissa into his arms and embraced her tightly. Unknowingly the priestesses of Sekhmet had reached across centuries to damn him again, for their curse was ruining his chance for love once more. What had he done to deserve such unhappiness? How could he bear it?

Suddenly the ship lurched so hard that they were flung off the bed. Asheris scrambled to his feet and reached for Karissa. He helped her stand.

"What happened?" she exclaimed.

"Perhaps we hit something." Asheris released her and stepped to the porthole between the bed and the door to the bathroom. He looked out at the whitecaps in the river, whipped up by the severe wind. "I believe we have run aground."

She scampered up behind him and wrapped her arms around his torso. Before he could reach up to touch her, he heard the captain of the vessel make an announcement over the intercom.

"All passengers and crew, report immediately to the upper deck. I repeat, report immediately to the upper deck."

Then the announcement was repeated in a variety of other languages.

A loud, metallic yawn split the air, and the ship listed to the side, remaining at an angle so severe that Asheris found it hard to keep his footing. He clutched Karissa's arm to keep her from falling. Her eyes were wide with fright.

"Asheris!" she cried. "Is the ship sinking?"

"It is probably just taking on water. Hurry and dress." He pressed a kiss to her lips. "You've got to get up to the lifeboats."

"What about you?" she asked, reaching for her underwear.

"I must go below and retrieve the crate."

"No, Asheris!" She grabbed at him, but he slipped past her and snatched up his pile of clothing.

"It's too dangerous," she cried. "You could be killed!"

"I must go. Hurry, now, Karissa!"

He yanked on his pants and left her calling at him to come back.

Asheris retraced his steps of a few hours ago, only this time the path was made difficult by the listing ship. By the time he reached the lower deck, he had to wade through shin-deep water. That meant the hold was probably submerged. He pulled open the door that led to the companionway into the hold. Fortunately, the door was on the high side of the listing ship, which allowed him a view of the watery expanse of the cargo area. Most of the freight the ship carried was too heavy to float. But a few barrels and crates bobbed on the surface, shadows on the glinting water. Asheris narrowed his eyes, searching in the gloom for one particular wooden box. He spotted it fifteen meters away, near a cluster of barrels.

Without a second thought, Asheris ran down the stairs and plunged into the cold water, praying the ship wouldn't roll before he could get to the crate. He feared being entombed in the watery depths of the Nile and wondered vaguely what would happen to the spirit panther should it be trapped underwater as well.

A few minutes later he grabbed the rope handle of Senefret's crate and turned to tow it back to the stairs. The ship screamed again, louder this time, as iron and steel twisted under the weight of the huge vessel. The hold tilted and the water covered up the last of the small portholes near the ceiling. Asheris pushed himself to swim harder, faster, but the weight of the wooden box dragged behind him. He thought of Karissa and pressed on.

At last, he felt the railing of the stairs and pulled himself up toward the angled door. He found the submerged stairs and used them for leverage as he hoisted the crate up the flooded companionway. The doorway proved a tight fit for the crate, but he managed to rotate it and wedge it through. He slid the crate up the corridor toward the next door, pushed it through and then struggled up the next set of stairs, walking half on the wall and half on the treads. The water dripping from his hair soon turned to sweat, both from the effort of dragging the box and the pressing need to get off the ship before it sank in the storm.

Finally, he got to the upper deck, only to find the crew still struggling with the lifeboats. Due to the angle of the deck, many of the boats were submerged and useless, the others too high to reach. Passengers and crew panicked all around him, running back and forth from the suspended lifeboats to the railing and screaming. The ship shuddered beneath his bare feet and lurched sideways. Asheris grabbed hold of the brass rail near the door and watched in horror as most of the untethered passengers careened across the deck and plunged into the choppy waters of the Nile. In the deepening dusk, Asheris saw crocodiles slide down the far bank and slip into the river. Frantic, he glanced around. Where was Karissa in the melee? He couldn't see her anywhere.

"Karissa!" he yelled into the gale. He swiped his hair off his forehead and called again as dread curled in the pit of his stomach. Had she fallen into the river with the rest of them? "Karissa!"

Swearing, he let go of the crate and stumbled to the rail. The crate slipped across the deck, hit the railing, and bounced end over end, sailing through the air and hitting the water with a smack. Asheris saw it disappear and then bob to the surface a few meters away. Luckily it hadn't struck anyone. The surface of the river churned with flailing, terrified people and floating debris. Behind them he could see the nearly indistinguishable bumps of the crocodiles as they swam closer.

Then he saw Karissa. She was vainly trying to reach a barrel but was continually thrown back by the waves in the water.

Though she was fighting to stay alive, she obviously didn't know how to swim. Soon she would tire, and the crocodiles would take her under.

Asheris looked back at the crate, which was floating downriver unaware of the crisis on the ship. He must make a choice and make it immediately. Either Karissa would die in the river, or he would lose Senefret's body forever. He hardly took a moment to consider, for he knew where his heart truly belonged. Though he might never be a whole man, he knew without a doubt that he loved Karissa Spencer and would give up his own life, his hopes and dreams and even Senefret's afterlife, to save her.

Bracing himself against the raging wind, he climbed onto the railing and jumped off.

With a smack, Asheris hit the water and went under. Up through the cold black river he swam, praying he would not be too late. He broke the surface with a gasp and looked around as water streamed into his eyes and a wave struck him in the face. Off to his right he glimpsed Karissa, just as she was sinking beneath the waves.

"No!" he shouted over the wind. He lunged forward and grabbed a handful of her hair as she disappeared in the current. With desperate hands, he cupped her chin and took off for the shore with swift sure strokes, knowing that within minutes the crocodiles would be upon them. Already he heard the terrified cries of the less fortunate as they were attacked by the reptiles.

He prayed to the gods that he would make it to the shore in time, not only to escape the crocodiles, but also to outrun the setting sun. Once he transformed into the panther, he would be of no help to Karissa, not in water. She was limp in his grip, and he wondered if she might already be dead. Distraught, he forced his arms and legs far beyond their limits, until his muscles screamed in agony. Still, he pressed onward, concentrating on the dim lights of the shoreline and telling himself that he was nearly there.

Nearly there. Nearly there. Nearly there.

At last, he felt the temperature of the water grow warmer, and then the smell of mud and reeds filled his nostrils. His free hand struck sand. He had made it! Asheris dragged himself to his feet, clutched Karissa under her arms and hauled her out of the water. His knees started to buckle before he made it all the way to the warm beach. Gasping for breath, he eased Karissa onto her stomach and then collapsed on the strip of land beside her.

After he recovered somewhat, he looked around, thankful that no crocodiles lounged on this small piece of sand. Then he checked Karissa to make certain she was breathing and comfortable. A pang of happiness washed over him. He had saved Karissa. She was alive. He was alive. That they had survived was a blessed miracle. He looked toward the river as the pang grew bittersweet.

Perhaps Senefret would one day understand the choice he'd had to make. He had chosen the living over the dead. There had been no alternative. Not for him.

Asheris reached out and lightly caressed Karissa's hair as he turned back to gaze at her delicate profile. He knew he would never tire of filling his eyes with her.

But there was nothing else he could do for her. His energy was completely drained. All he could do was pull her into his arms and wrap himself around her drenched body. He was tired beyond endurance. He couldn't walk another step. Perhaps a rescue crew would find them. Asheris lay his head on his arm. Then all went black as he lost consciousness.

He slept through the rest of the storm, the rest of the night, and didn't wake up until sunrise, when the sound of barking dogs startled him awake. Asheris jerked up, grimacing in pain at the stiffness in his muscles. He glanced at the sky, which was blue and clear, with no signs of the storm of the previous night. Then he gazed down at Karissa, still lying in the sand beside him, her cloud of black hair tangled around her shoulders.

As he lay there, he realized he was still dressed in his pants. He never returned from his forays as a panther without waking up completely naked. In fact, he had learned to remove his clothing at dusk, so that he wouldn't ruin or lose any of his apparel during the transformations. Why hadn't he lost the trousers last night?

Perplexed, Asheris glanced around at the sand. He couldn't spot a single panther track. There was no evidence whatsoever that he had been a panther during the night. In fact, he had awakened still wrapped around Karissa in the exact position he had assumed before falling asleep. That was impossible. Wasn't it?

A shudder rippled down Asheris' back as a startling possibility dawned on him. And yet, he found it impossible to believe the truth staring him in the face. He had remained a man the entire night. But how could that have occurred? The only way the curse could be lifted was by the hand of a woman who truly loved him. He had always assumed his destiny was linked to Senefret, that her love could cure him. But her love was forever out of reach now. And yet...

He stared at Karissa. Yesterday afternoon she had said that she loved him, but he hadn't connected the confession to the curse. Could it be true? Was he no longer cursed? Could he be a whole man at last, free of his wandering nights as a panther? Osiris, let it be so!

Just then the reeds above him parted and a dog's head poked through the blades. The basenji yapped and growled, waking Karissa. An instant later, Jamal's face appeared directly above them.

"Mr. Asher!" he exclaimed with a huge grin. "Allah be praised! We have found you!"

Just after noon, Karissa stood at the side of the Land Rover while a manservant put a small bag containing her scant wardrobe and toiletries in the back. Then she walked into the house to see if Asheris had finished his telephone conversation. She wanted to say good-bye to him in the garden and not at the airport, where they would be in full view of strangers.

She bid good-bye to Eisha and then turned as Asheris walked up, dressed in white. He looked radiantly handsome.

"You really are going?" he said in greeting, talking her hands in his tan ones. "I can't change your mind?"

"I wish I could stay, but all the arrangements have been made. I can't turn my back on my business. Surely you understand that, Asheris."

"Yes." He smiled sadly. "I understand. But that does not mean that I like your decision." He pulled her closer, and she nestled against him, feeling as she had felt from the very first that their bodies had been molded to fit together as one. He gazed down at her and smiled, which was highly infectious. She knew she was grinning back, unable to control the joy she felt in his arms. He had sacrificed a great deal to save her life, and his sacrifice meant the world to her.

"I'll come back," she promised. "As soon as I can."

"Tomorrow?" he urged, kissing her with longing and passion. She smiled beneath the kiss, and he rose from her mouth. "How can I endure the hours until you are back in my arms?"

"I promise it won't be long."

"Good. Because you are part of me, Karissa."

She gazed up at him. It was true. A strong bond bound them together, unspoken, unbroken, undeniable. Only one thing marred the joy of the moment. Though Asher had saved her life and had given up Senefret's crate, he still had not admitted that he loved her.

She touched his cheek. "Asheris, why don't you just come with me?"

"I would, but for the call I just received."

"And?"

"It seems a fisherman found my crate."

"Oh." Karissa felt a twinge of disquiet that she instantly pushed aside. If Asheris could countenance her leaving for the PBS interview, she could countenance his efforts to give Senefret a proper burial. She forced a smile. "You'll phone me, won't you, once you find out what's in that little cedar box?"

"Of course. I will call you every day, just to hear your voice."

He kissed her again, embracing her until the manservant appeared and discreetly suggested that it was time they leave for the airport.

"Just a moment," Asheris said, stepping back but keeping her hand in his. "There is something I want to do while you are still here."

"Yes?" Karissa glanced up at him in surprise.

"I have been thinking about personal freedom very much lately."

"Yes?" She still didn't comprehend what he was getting at.

Asheris walked to the nearest birdcage and lifted the latch on the door. "At one time I thought these birds were beautiful and fascinating to watch. But now I see them only as pitiful hostages."

Karissa's heart swelled with love for Asheris as she looked at the falcons sitting on the perch. She knew why he had been fascinated with birds. He was part cat in his soul. The only thing she didn't understand was why his fascination for birds should suddenly change.

"I thought I was protecting them," he continued, "when all the time I have been keeping them from living their natural lives."

"Safety isn't what makes life worth living," she replied. "I've learned that lesson well enough."

He glanced down at her. "That's why I thought you might like to see the birds set free before you go."

"I would," Karissa said, as tears came to her eyes. Asheris had set her free of her past, of her guilt. And she would always love him for it.

Asheris opened door after door, and the birds took wing, soaring over the garden like angels spiraling to the sun. One of the falcons rose above their heads and circled the garden, crying out a haunting call of scree, scree.

Karissa shaded her eyes and watched the birds as Asheris stood behind her and wrapped his arms around her.

"They will come back to my garden," he said softly into her hair, "of their own free will. I am certain of it."

She nodded and rested her head against his chest, reveling in his wonderful combination of strength and sensitivity. Just like the birds, she would return to Asheris, too, back to his garden and the man she had come to love with all her heart.

Chapter Eleven

B*altimore, Maryland*

Karissa heard a prying sound in the back of the gallery and put aside her wine glass. She was quite certain she was the only person remaining after the film crew had left. Even Josh had waved good-bye and had gone to have a drink with one of the blond make-up artists.

"Who's there?" Karissa called, tiredly rising from the chair where she had been interviewed. The filming had taken two days and she was exhausted. But her spirits were dragging more than her body, for Asheris had not called her once since she had flown back to Baltimore. Something had happened to him, or he had decided to forget her. Either possibility devastated her.

She walked toward the rear of the building. "Who's there?" she called again.

No one answered.

She peered into the darkness, wishing she would have turned on the lights. And then she saw them—two golden eyes gazing at her from out of the gloom. Her voice caught in her throat, and her heart began to pound furiously.

"Ebony," a low voice rumbled near the back door. "If you sculpt a cat in ebony, you will find satisfaction."

She couldn't believe her eyes or her ears.

"Asheris?" she whispered.

He stepped out from behind a wooden crate and held out his arms. He was dressed in his long black coat and gloves. She had never seen a more beautiful sight in her entire life. With a cry of joy, she vaulted into his embrace.

After a long hug and an even longer kiss, Asheris pulled away from her mouth. "Look what I have brought for you," he said, pushing aside the lid of the crate.

Karissa glanced at the contents of the box. In the shadows, she could see nothing but a dark lump. "What is it?"

"Ebony," he declared proudly. "For your next and best sculpture."

"How can you be so sure? I haven't been successful yet in capturing the spirit of the panther."

"Ah, but this time you will."

"Why do you say that?"

Asheris held her close. "Because the panther spirit is no longer trapped within me. It is free to be captured by your hands and brought to life in the wood I have brought you."

"Asheris!" Karissa stepped back and raked him with a critical inspection. "What are you saying? You are no longer under the curse?"

"No. Your love freed me, Karissa." He smiled, his teeth flashing in the darkness. "I am a new man!"

"But why didn't you say so before? Before I left Egypt?"

"I was not certain then. I had to see if the night belonged to the panther or to me. And I was reluctant to mention it to you in case my hopes soared too high. Then when I found out for certain, I longed to tell you myself in person, not on the telephone."

His silence of the last two days was instantly forgiven. She grinned and hugged him tightly, wondering what it could mean for the two of them. Was he whole now, whole enough to give himself completely to her? Or did part of him still belong to Senefret?

"There is more, Karissa," he said, stroking her hair.

"Yes?"

"I barely know how to begin." He laughed and looked down at her, and his face was full of joy. She had never heard him laugh before and the sound brought tears to her eyes.

"Come. Sit down and tell me," she urged, pulling him by the hand to the interview set. She sat upon the upholstered chair, but he remained on his feet and paced back and forth in front of her.

"Well?" Karissa asked, dying of curiosity.

He glanced at her and smiled again. Then he pulled off his gloves and stuffed them into the pockets of his overcoat.

"Do you recall that small cedar box?" he inquired.

"Of course."

He reached into the inner pocket of his coat and drew out a folded paper. "Inside the box was this letter to me. From Senefret."

"What?" Karissa thought she hadn't heard him correctly.

"Yes. Senefret was the one who broke into the tomb, left the box, and then resealed the entrance."

"Senefret?"

Asheris nodded, his eyes alight.

"But I thought it was her tomb. Her mummy."

Asheris nodded again. "So did everyone. When in fact, the mummy was the body of a young priestess who had died of a wasting disease at the same time Senefret was to be executed. She was entombed in place of Senefret."

"Why?"

"To fool the pharaoh. For you see, Senefret escaped the Temple of Sekhmet, leaving the priestesses with no one to punish, no one to offer as sacrifice to my half-brother."

"Senefret escaped?"

Asheris grinned. "Senefret was resourceful. She left the box there, hoping someday I would return to Thebes, perhaps break into her tomb, and find the letter she had written to me."

"So, if she wasn't killed, what happened to her?"

"She fled to the outer provinces."

His eyes gleamed as he sat down next to Karissa. "How I wish I had known all of this. I have spent an eternity grieving for Senefret, when all the time she was never in the Valley of the Damned at all."

Karissa stared at him in shock. Then she reached out a trembling hand. "May I see the letter?" she asked.

"It is a copy," he said, giving it to her. "And translated into English so that you can read it."

His thoughtfulness never ceased to amaze her. She scanned the text, which explained most of what he already told her. At the bottom of the page, however, were words that tugged at her heart.

"I know of no other way to contact you, my heart, for to be seen with you would mean certain death for both of us, and I could never put your life in danger. I only hope that someday you will come to know that I live for you, if not in this lifetime, perhaps through my daughter, and her daughter after her, and so on. A love such as ours was destined to endure."

Karissa looked up from the letter to find Asheris studying her intently. She frowned. "How do you know this is genuine?"

she asked. "How do you know it wasn't a cruel joke and that the mummy really was Senefret?"

"There was one way to find out," Asheris replied grimly. "Senefret was cursed by the priestesses of Sekhmet and marked with a special brand on her neck. When I unwrapped the mummy, I found no such mark. Had it been there, it should have been evident, even after thousands of years."

A chill coursed through Karissa. "What kind of mark was it, exactly?"

"A red spot in the shape of a cat, to identify that she belonged to the Temple of Sekhmet."

Karissa was so shocked, she dropped the letter. It fluttered to the floor, but she took no notice.

"Karissa, what is wrong?"

"I have such a mark," Karissa whispered, slowly rising to her feet. "So did my grandmother Menmet and her mother before her."

"A mark in the shape of a cat?"

"Yes."

"Where?"

"Here." Karissa pulled back her hair into a ponytail and lifted it off her neck. She rotated to display her back to Asheris. "See there at the base of my hairline?"

He stepped closer. "I do not believe it," he exclaimed.

"I was told it's a family birthmark."

She felt Asheris' warm touch on her neck as he outlined the shape of the cat with his index finger. Then he slowly turned her around and regarded her, his eyes dark and probing.

"You never mentioned your mark."

"There was no reason to." She stared up at him, realizing the impact this had on both of them. Could she belong to the same family as Senefret? Could she be genetically linked to the beautiful priestess who had captured Asheris' heart? Could she possibly be made of the same essence of woman as the Senefret of long ago?

"Oh, God, Asheris!" she gasped. "Could it be that—"

"Yes!" he exclaimed, squeezing the tops of her arms. "You are of her lineage. That explains everything—the way I was drawn to you, the way you spoke to my heart, the way I've been in love with you from the very first."

"You're in love with me?"

"Yes, but I could never tell you. How could I? I was not whole. I was half-panther, half-man, and half-devoted to a woman I thought long dead." He laughed and squeezed her again, "But she is in you as surely as you are standing here!"

"You love me."

"I love you as surely as the sun rises in the east." He embraced her, crushing her in joy. "Ah, Karissa, I love you boundlessly, hopelessly, eternally."

She felt her heart blossoming with happiness, the likes of which she had never known. In that moment she knew why she had the mark, why the land of Nile had always called to her, and why this man had become part of her heart in so many ways in such a short time. Her blood was the blood of the priestess, flowing through eternity toward Lord Azhur as the Nile had flowed to the sea since time began.

"I come from an ancient line," she murmured near his ear. "I'd like to explore that heritage."

"The only way to do that is to come back to Egypt," he replied. "And employ the services of an expert."

"And who might that be?" she teased.

"Though I dislike braggarts," he said, "I must admit that I am the best."

"Yes, you are." She hugged him fiercely.

"And if you can be persuaded to travel with me again, I have two tickets for luxury accommodations on the Cairo Queen leaving New York in four days."

"Another ship?" she asked, arching one eyebrow.

"I rather enjoyed our voyage before we hit the sandbar." Asheris kissed the tip of her nose. "And I thought you might like a longer trip this time."

"As long as you don't have any crates with you."

"No more crates, my love," he replied. "I am finished with the past now. All I want is the future. With you in it."

"A little bit of here and now wouldn't be so bad either," she said, pulling him down to her mouth.

"Mmm," he mumbled, drawing her against his body.

"Are you sure you are no longer a panther," she asked, kissing his cheek. "Not even a tiny bit?"

"What do you have in mind?"

She whispered her request in his ear.

He growled.

Author's Note

During the research for this story, I turned up some fascinating facts about ancient and modern Egypt, including a new theory regarding construction techniques of the pyramids and the mystery surrounding the sphinx. Not even experts are certain as to the purpose of the Great Sphinx that guards the pyramids on the Giza Plateau.

Is the monument merely ornamental? What lies beneath it? Is there a sealed chamber full of treasure? Are there hidden tunnels? If so, where do they lead? As of the writing of this book (1994), excavation beneath the sphinx is still prohibited.

Some scientists claim that the Great Sphinx is much older than we think—built 10,000 years ago, not 4000—and that rain eroded the limestone blocks, not wind and sand. This tells us that Egypt may have once been a lush, tropical land. The water erosion theory is considered fringe by other scientists. But it's that kind of theory that stokes my "what-if" imagination.

Not being able to leave such mysteries lie, I decided to write a sequel to this book in which I explore a similar sphinx in Luxor, while uncovering the startling secret of the Spencer family in The Lost Goddess.

Find out more at https://patriciasimpson.com/books/lost-goddess

2023 Addendum

This book was written before the universal adoption of cell phones. No one in Lord of the Nile carries a mobile phone or uses Twitter. How our lives have changed...

Don't miss out!

Visit the website below and you can sign up to receive emails whenever Patricia Simpson publishes a new book. There's no charge and no obligation.

https://books2read.com/r/B-A-EZJM-NVCHC

BOOKS 2 READ

Connecting independent readers to independent writers.

Also by Patricia Simpson

Black Panther Series
Lord of the Nile

The Londo Chronicles
Apothecary
Phoenix
Prodigy

Watch for more at https://patriciasimpson.com.

About the Author

Patricia Simpson is a bestselling writer from the Bay Area of California. She has won numerous awards, including multiple Reviewer's Choice Awards from Romantic Times as well as a Career Achievement Award. One of her more recent novels, SPELLBOUND, was nominated Best Indie Paranormal of the Year. After a long career with TOR, Silhouette and HarperMonogram, Patricia is now enjoying creative freedom as an indie author.

Read more at https://patriciasimpson.com.